Bawdy Tales from the Courts of Medieval France

Bawdy Tales
from the
Courts of Medieval France

Translated and Edited by

PAUL BRIANS

HARPER TORCHBOOKS
HARPER & ROW, PUBLISHERS
NEW YORK • EVANSTON • SAN FRANCISCO • LONDON

First HARPER TORCHBOOK edition published 1973.

LIBRARY OF CONGRESS CATALOG CARD NUMBER: 72–6316

STANDARD BOOK NUMBER: 06–131725–X

Contents

Introduction

Not so very many years ago, an anthology of this sort would have required an apology rather than an introduction. Even now some medievalists, mostly in the thrall of nineteenth-century scholarship, are anxious to defend their interest in bawdy tales by pointing out that they are invaluable sources of folklore, of information about Oriental influences on European literature, of realistic slices of bourgeois life, and so forth. The fact that these are delightfully entertaining and enjoyable tales in their own right is left unmentioned.

When I was introduced to a freshman coed once as a "medievalist," she said she didn't know much about the period. "Wasn't that when they wrote the Bible and all that kind of stuff?" she asked. Without suggesting that the average person is quite that unaware of the Middle Ages, I suspect that for many people the medieval *Zeitgeist* is more Dantesque than Chaucerian. Chaucer, after all, came late, imitating and borrowing from Boccaccio, a Renaissance writer. The Renaissance is the great age of the bawdy tale, as everyone knows. From Boccaccio to Marguerite de Navarre, the voluminous collections poured out, breaking through the pious gloom of the Middle Ages.

Only it isn't true, of course. The Renaissance novella is a direct descendant of the medieval fabliau. The real flowering of the

genre had taken place in the twelfth century. As a teller of bawdy
tales, Boccaccio is rather derivative. Forced by his scheme in the
Decameron to recount an inordinate number of tales, he seems
not to have spent too much time on any single one. The medieval
fableor was less of an anthologist-craftsman and more of an artist.
The stories were told one at a time for their own sake and were
often composed with literary skill of a very high order. Their main
distinction lay in their extensive use of dialogue to create lively
characterizations. While many Renaissance novellas are more polished in style, the medieval fabliaux are often more vivid and
dramatic.

One of the purposes of this small anthology is to reveal the very
great skill and craftsmanship to be found in these medieval tales.
In addition, I do have a point to make. Stated simply, it is this:
the love of bawdy stories knows no class boundaries.

It may surprise some that such a statement should have to be
made, but it does have to be made. Some medievalists not only
cling to nineteenth-century ideals of scholarship, but they cling to
the moral standards of the nineteeth century as well. They are
capable of being sincerely shocked by "obscene writing," though
medieval bawdry is quite tame compared to what is freely available
on the newsstands today. Seemingly unaware of the society around
them reading *Evergreen Review* and the underground papers and
watching Swedish films, they voice their astonishment at the lewd
twelfth century and exclaim over medieval man's lack of natural
modesty. What could be tolerated then is intolerable now, they
say, and they are careful to warn their readers accordingly. They
still live in the world of the asterisk and the prudish ellipsis.

There have always been some scholars who were disturbed by
the abundance of what they consider to be obscene matter in
medieval literature. Joseph Bédier, in his classic study of the
fabliaux written at the turn of the century, noted that bawdry

intruded into every literary genre, almost without exception.* He exclaimed at the "promiscuity" of the medieval public for these tales and shuddered at the realization that even women's chaste ears were occasionally subjected to them. In the end, however, Bédier took refuge in the theory which gave comfort to most nineteenth-century scholars: bawdy tales were a product of the bourgeoisie, and they were mostly confined to that vulgar class. According to this theory, the nobility were delighted instead by high-minded epics and romances and delicate allegories of love. If a *jongleur* was occasionally called upon to recite a fabliau to a group of lords in their cups once the ladies had been dismissed, that was understandable, if not altogether excusable. (Bédier clearly envisions this aspect of medieval life as a nineteenth-century bourgeois dinner party.)

The fabliaux are bourgeois literature, according to Bédier and others, as are the farces and the tales of Renart, the fox. They are listed as such in the standard bibliographies. In 1957 Per Nykrog challenged this view in his revolutionary work on the fabliaux.** Unlike Bédier, Nykrog is a product of the twentieth century, quite willing to face the evidence without blushing. He found that not only did the nobility enjoy fabliaux, but that fabliaux were often written for and by them. Bédier had regretfully admitted the "contamination" of noble genres by the lewd fabliau spirit. Nykrog showed that bawdry was not the exclusive possession of the lower classes and that its persistent identification with bourgeois authors had little basis in fact.

It makes sense, as most of us are beginning to recognize. Bawdy stories, even pornography, have historically been more the property of the nobility than of the bourgeoisie. No one is surprised to

* *Les Fabliaux: Etudes de littérature populaire et d'histoire littéraire du moyen âge*, 5th ed., rev. and corr. (Paris: Champion, 1925).

** *Les Fabliaux: Etude d'histoire littéraire et de stylistique médiévale* (Copenhague: E. Munksgaard, 1957).

find Brantôme amusing the Renaissance French court; why should they be surprised at the presence of *fableors* in medieval French castles? After all, prudishness is more a bourgeois than a noble trait.

To prove that noble interest in fabliaux was not mere literary slumming, I have also translated a number of tales distinctly noble in milieu and subject matter which are quite as explicit, quite as bawdy, and quite as entertaining as the so-called bourgeois stories. They illustrate as clearly as anything could that the medieval world was not divided between the pious, high-minded court and the lusty, low-minded town. They also illustrate that bawdy tales can be told with wit, skill, and grace.

Note on the Translations

All of the tales here translated were originally composed in verse, the standard narrative medium of the earlier Middle Ages. If their authors were living today, almost all of them would undoubtedly write in prose. Our modern languages with their rigidified syntax and low tolerance for ambiguity cannot satisfactorily render the free-wheeling, double-jointed phrases which make up medieval verse narrative. I have therefore chosen prose as my medium. Occasionally something is lost, but few of the authors of these tales are outstanding versifiers, and often more is gained by the increased clarity of prose. The only truly successful English verse translation of a bawdy tale is the delightful version of "The Knight Who Made Cunts and Assholes Speak" (that is the actual title, the translators call it "The Knight Who Conjured Voices") in Hellman and O'Gorman's anthology.* If their translation had not been so masterful, I would have included the tale here, for it is an exceptionally striking example of noble bawdry.

I have tried to avoid translating awkward constructions literally and have left out repetitions and tags when they were obviously meant only to fill out a line. A plethora of "*moults*," weak, almost meaningless intensifiers, has been omitted. Since many of the tales

* Robert Hellman and Richard O'Gorman, trans., *Fabliaux: Ribald Tales from the Old French* (New York: Crowell, 1965).

contain a great deal of dialogue, I have tried to avoid too many annoying archaisms and have occasionally taken slight liberties to modernize the speech forms. As a rule, however, my translations are very close and, as much as possible, literal. I have faithfully translated all Old French obscenities by the appropriate modern English obscenities and have equally used English circumlocutions for French circumlocutions. There has been no censoring or editing of any of the tales.

As a final note, it may be helpful to point out that I have adhered to the medieval forms of address. "Sire" is said to a nobleman, a superior. "Vassal" is used to address a social inferior and occurs occasionally in these tales as a term of insult. English "Sir" translates French "messire," so that "messire Gauvain" is translated as "Sir Gawain."

Bawdy Tales from the Courts of Medieval France

The Knight of the Sword

Let him who loves delight and joy come forward; listen and hear an adventure which happened to a good knight who kept loyalty, prowess, and honor; and let him come who never loved a cowardly, false, or base man. I tell of Sir Gawain, who was so knowledgeable and whose valor in arms was so praiseworthy that it could never be told or known. Whoever would go over and summarize all his virtues would never finish; but if I cannot go over them all, I should not therefore remain silent.

In my opinion, Chrétien de Troyes—who told of King Arthur, of his court and company, which was so famed and praised, and who told the deeds of others—should not be blamed. And yet he told no tale of him, and he was too fine a man to forget.* Therefore I should like to recount an adventure which happened to that good knight.

King Arthur was at his city of Cardoil one spring, and with him were the Queen and Gawain, Kay the Seneschal, and Ivain, along with just twenty of the others. One day Gawain felt the desire to go out and divert himself, so he had his horse readied and dressed

SOURCE: Edward Cooke Armstrong, ed., *Le Chevalier à L'Epée: An Old French Poem* (Baltimore, Md.: John Murphy, 1900).
* While Chrétien left no tale completely devoted to the knight, his *Perceval* or *Roman del Graal* contains a long adventure of Gawain within it.

himself nobly. He put gold spurs on his cut-off boots, worked with silken cloth. He also wore leggings—very white and strong, a short, wide shirt, finely pleated linen, and a fur mantle. He was indeed richly dressed.

Then he went out of the city, keeping to the road until he entered the forest. He listened to the song of the birds, who sang so sweetly. He listened until he had heard enough, then entered into thoughts of an adventure which had happened to him. He remained so long in thought that he wandered in the forest and lost his way. The sun began to sink, and he began to think. Night was falling when he emerged from his thoughts, but he had no idea where he was.

He thought he would turn back, but entered into a pathway that led ever onward before him. It continued to get darker, and he still didn't know where to go. He looked before him, down a path through a clearing in a thicket, and saw a great fire lit. He headed that way, for he thought he would find someone to show him his way: a woodcutter or a charcoal burner.

Then he saw a horse next to the fire, tied to a tree. He went up to the fire and saw a knight sitting. Immediately he greeted him. "May the Lord," he said, "who made the world and placed our souls and bodies in it, give you, sir, of His bounty."

"Friend," he said, "may God keep you. Tell me where you have come from, traveling alone at such an hour."

Gawain told him everything, the truth, from beginning to end— how he had gone out for amusement and how he had wandered, absorbed in thought, until he had lost his way. The knight told him that if he would wait until morning he would gladly put him back on his way, but only if he would remain with him and bear him company until the night had passed. This wish was granted. He put down his lance and shield, got off his horse, tied it to a bush, covered himself with his mantle, and sat down by the fire.

The knight asked him how he had wandered that day, and

Gawain told him everything without lying. But the knight deceived him, for he uttered not a word of truth. You will hear the reason he did this.

When they had stayed awake long enough and talked of various matters, they fell asleep by the fire. At daybreak, first Sir Gawain, then the knight, awoke. "My house is quite near here—not more than two leagues. I invite you to come. You will have fine lodging."

They mounted their horses, took up their shields, their lances, and their swords, and started off on a beaten path. They had not traveled far before they emerged from the forest into a plain.

The knight spoke to him: "Sire, listen to me. It is always the custom that, if a courteous and wise knight brings another with him, he should go before him to have his lodging prepared, so that those not expecting him should be ready and he should not find anything to displease him. I have no one to send ahead, as you can see; I am alone. If you please, continue on at your leisure, and I shall hurry ahead. You will see my house in an enclosure up ahead by a valley."

Gawain knew well that what he had said was correct and proper, so he slowed his pace and the other raced ahead.

Sir Gawain came upon four shepherds who had stopped beside the road. He greeted them courteously, and they returned his greeting in the name of God. Then he went on by them and spoke no further to them.

"Alas!" said one. "Curse the day! Good knight, noble and skilled, it certainly isn't right that you should be wounded or injured." Gawain, who heard these words, was amazed. He wondered greatly why he was being lamented for, when he knew nothing of it.

He turned back quickly and greeted them. Politely he asked them to tell him truly why they had said "Curse the day." One answered, "Sire, we pity you because of what we see you following.

We have seen that knight who went by on his horse ahead of you lead off many knights, but we have never yet seen one return."

Gawain said, "Friend, do you know that he does them anything other than good?"

"Sire, in this country, they say that whenever a man contradicts him in anything, whether for evil or for good, he has him killed in his lodging. We know this only from hearsay, for we have never yet seen a man who came back from there. If you will believe us, you won't follow a step further, if you care for your life. You are such a fine knight, that it would be too bad if he killed you."

Gawain said to them, "Shepherds, I commend you to God. I do not wish, on a boy's word, to stay out of his land. If it should be known in a man's own country that he had held back for so little, he would be forever reproached."

While he was thinking, his horse ambled on as he had taught it from there to the valley. Near a great enclosure he saw a lovely castle on a hillock of new farmland. He saw that the moat was wide and deep and that in the enclosure across the bridge there was a fine lodging. He had never in his life seen such a fine lodging, whether belonging to a prince or to a king. I don't want to spend time describing the lodging, but it was very lovely and fine.

He came up to the palisade and went through the gate, passing into the enclosed area, to the end of the bridge. The lord ran out to him, pretending to be very happy at his coming.

A boy took his arms, another took his horse, and a third removed his spurs. Then his host took him by the hand and led him across the bridge. They found a fine fire in the hall in front of the tower, with fine seats around it, covered with purple silk. They stabled his horse apart and brought it an abundance of oats and hay.

Gawain thanked him for everything, not wishing to contradict him in anything. His host said, "Good sir, the servants are hastening to prepare the meal, so amuse yourself for a while. Enjoy yourself and make yourself comfortable. If anything displeases you, say so."

Gawain said that everything in the lodging was just as he wished.

The lord went into the chamber to look for his daughter, who was more precious than any girl in the whole world. I could never tell you all, or even half, of the beauty with which she was endowed and graced. I don't want to pass over it, but I will tell you in a few words that in her was assembled all that nature can provide of courtesy and beauty which is pleasing to man.

The host, who was no boor, took her by the right hand and led her into the hall. Gawain, who was stunned by her great beauty, nevertheless sprang to his feet. The girl was even more amazed when she saw Gawain's good looks and fine clothing, but nevertheless she courteously and briefly greeted him.

Then he gave her hand to Gawain and said to him, "I bring you my daughter, so you shall not be bored, for I have no finer entertainment to present to you. If she wishes, she can bear you fine company. I hope she will wish to, for you are so wise and valorous that if she fell in love with you, it would only be an honor to me. I give you my place as a gift and will not be jealous of you. So I command her here before you not to deny you anything."

Gawain thanked him politely, not wishing to contradict him, and he went quickly to the kitchen to see if they could dine soon. Gawain, worried about the host, whom he greatly feared, nevertheless sat down by the maiden and courteously and faultlessly conversed with the blond-haired girl. She said neither too much nor too little and talked with him intelligently. He offered her his service and told her so much of what he felt that she, who was intelligent and wise, saw and heard quite well that he would like, more than anything else, to please her. Then she did not know what to do—whether to deny or to grant. He could speak so courteously, and she perceived that he had so many good qualities, that she fell deeply in love with him, if only she had dared to reveal it to him.

But she would not, for anything in the world, grant him something when he could not go on to take more. She knew that she would be acting badly if she caused him the pain of love when he would never attain the goal. But refusing grieved her, so much was her heart moved toward him. So she spoke courteously, "Sire, I heard my father demand that I do anything that might delight you. But I tell you from my own knowledge that if I granted you your will, you would come to no good end; rather, I would have murdered and betrayed you. I warn you of one thing in good faith—keep yourself from villainy, and do not contradict my father in anything he may say, for good or for evil, or you will be immediately killed. And don't behave as if you knew any of this."

Then the host, who had gone to the kitchen, returned; and the meal was prepared. He ordered water, not wanting to delay. When they had washed, they sat down and the servants put the napkins on the fine white tablecloths with salt-cellars and knives, then the bread, then the wine in cups of silver and fine gold. But I don't want to linger, describing the courses one by one. They had a lot of flesh and fish, roasted fowl and venison, and they ate with great pleasure. The host strongly urged Gawain and the maiden to drink and told the maiden to urge on the knight and said to him, "You should be proud that I wish her to befriend you." Gawain thanked him politely.

When they had eaten well, the servants removed the tablecloths and napkins and towels to be cleaned. The host said after the meal that he wished to go look over his woods and asked Gawain to sit down and amuse himself with the girl. Then he called Gawain and told him and commanded him not to leave until he returned, and he ordered a servant—if he should make any suspicious move—to seize him immediately.

Gawain, who was wise and courteous, saw clearly that he must remain, and that it could not be otherwise. So he said quickly that he had no desire to go, for he wished to lodge there. The host mounted his horse and rode swiftly off, searching for another adventure, for he was sure of this one closed within his walls.

Gawain took the girl by the hand and they sat down to devise how he could protect himself. She gently comforted him, but she was worried and in despair because she didn't know what her father's will was. If she had known it, she would have showed him how he could escape. But he didn't want to say anything about it; so he should keep from contradicting him and escape, if he could, in that way.

"Let this be," he said. "He won't do me any harm. He brought me to his castle and was very courteous to me. Neither now or in the future, as long as he honors me and acts well toward me, will I fear anything, until I know and see any reason to fear him."

She said, "There's no need for that. As many men say, one should praise the day at evening, when one sees that its end is good. Thus should one judge his host in the morning. May God grant, as I desire, that you may part from your host joyfully, without misfortune."

When they had spoken at length of one thing and another, the host returned home. Gawain and the girl, holding hands, sprang to their feet and greeted him politely. He told them that he had hurried, for he feared that, if he delayed, Gawain would leave. Thus he had delayed no longer.

Night began to fall, and the host ordered his servants to prepare supper. He said to his daughter, "You may amuse yourself by ordering wine and fruit, but nothing else, for you ate quite a lot before."

Then he gave his orders, washed, and had the fruit set before them. The servants brought an abundance of many kinds of wine. "Sire, be of good cheer," he said to Sir Gawain. "One thing you may be sure of: it bothers and disturbs me if I have a guest who doesn't look out for himself and say what he wants."

"Sire, to tell the truth," said Gawain, "I'm quite happy."

When they had eaten the fruit, the host ordered the beds made up and said, "I shall lie here outside, and this knight shall lie in my bed. It is not a little thing I do, for my daughter shall lie with him. I think she is well occupied with such a fine knight."

She should have been very happy with what he had granted them. Both of them thanked him and acted as if they were greatly pleased. But Gawain was very uneasy, for he feared that if he went to bed he would have him chopped up; and he knew very well that if he contradicted him, he would kill him.

The host hurried them to bed; he took her by the hand and led her straight into the chamber. The sweet-faced girl went with him. The chamber was well-curtained; a dozen candles burned there all around the bed, giving a great light. The bed was finely made up with rich covers and white sheets. But I don't want to delay describing the richness of the imported silken drapes from Palermo and Romania with which the room was decorated—and sables in various shades of gray. Briefly, there was great abundance of whatever should grace knights and ladies both in winter and summer. There were many rich furnishings. Gawain marveled at the richness he saw.

The knight said to him, "This room is very fine. You and the girl will lie here and nowhere else. My girl, close the door and do his will, for I know that such people hardly need urging. But I would like to warn you not to put out the candles, for that would really anger me. I order this because I want him to see your great beauty as you lie in his arms. Thus he will have more delight, and you will see his fine body."

Then he left the room and the girl closed the door. Sir Gawain got into bed; she came to the bed and lay down by him, nude. There was no need to ask her. All that night she lay gently in his arms. He kissed and embraced her often, and went so far that he was about to do his will when she said, "Sire, please, it can't go on this way. I am not unguarded here with you."

Gawain looked all around, but saw not a living thing. "My sweet," he said, "I would like to ask you to tell me who prevents me from doing my will with you."

She answered, "I'll willingly tell you what I know. Do you see that sword hanging there by the silver cord, with the pommel and hilt of fine gold? I am not merely guessing at what you will hear me tell you now; I have seen it proven. My father loves it dearly, for he has often killed many fine knights with it. You should know that it has killed here alone more than twenty. I don't know where he got it, but no knight who has ever entered this door has escaped alive. My father pretends to like them, but for the slightest fault, he will kill them. They must refrain from villainy. They have to stick to the straight and narrow. Now you have learned the rule. If the guest does nothing wrong and guards himself so well that he isn't caught by anything, then at night he is put to bed with me. There he goes to his death.

"Let me tell you why none escapes. If he makes any semblance of a move to do it to me, immediately the sword pierces him through the body; and if he wants to reach toward it to take and remove it, it leaps out of its scabbard and strikes him through the body. The truth is that the sword is enchanted in such a way that it always guards me. Before, I wouldn't have protected you; but you are so courteous and wise that it would be too bad, and the thought of it would always oppress me if you were to be killed because of me."

Then Gawain didn't know what to do. He had never heard a greater threat in all his life, and he suspected that she spoke in order to protect herself, so that he wouldn't take his pleasure with her. On the other hand he thought that it could not be hidden— it would be known everywhere—that he had lain alone, nude with

her in her bed and had refrained from taking his pleasure solely
because of what she said. It is better to die with honor than to live
long in shame.

"My dear," he said, "that doesn't matter. Since I have gone this
far, I want to really become your lover. There is no way you can
get out of it."

"Don't blame me from now on," she said. Then he approached
closer so that she screamed; and the blade sprang out of its scabbard and struck him right along the side, removing some flesh; but
it didn't wound him severely. It pierced through the covers and
the sheets to the straw mattress, then leaped back into its scabbard. Gawain lay shocked, having lost all desire. He lay by her
quite stunned.

"Sire," she said, "for God's sake; you thought that I told you
this to defend myself from you, but I have never told any other
knight except you about it. In fact, I am astonished that you were
not immediately and infallibly struck dead at the first blow. For
God's sake, lie in peace and be careful to keep from touching me
in any way. A wise man quickly understands something that is
turning out badly for him."

Gawain remained pensive and mournful, for he didn't know
how he could contain himself. If, by God's will, he should ever
return to his land, and the thing were not concealed but known
everywhere—that he had lain alone at night with a comely, beautiful maiden but had done nothing with her and that nothing
prevented him except the threat of a sword which was not even
held by anyone—he would be forever disgraced if she thus escaped
him.

He was distressed by the candles he saw around him which shed
a bright light by which he saw her great beauty. Her face was pale
and smooth and her eyebrows delicate, her eyes green, her nose
well-placed—a fresh and rosy face, a little laughing mouth, a long
and comely neck, long arms and white hands, and soft, smooth

flanks: beneath the sheets, white tender skin. No one could have criticized anything in her, so well was her body assembled and made.

He gently drew near her, unlike a base-born man; and he would certainly have played the game with her then, when the sword leaped out of its scabbard and again attacked him. The flat of it struck him on the neck. He almost lost his wits, but the sword wavered a little; it turned into his right shoulder, slicing off three inches of flesh, and struck into the silk cover, slicing off a piece of it. Then it stuck itself back into its scabbard.

When Gawain felt himself wounded in the shoulder and in the side and saw that he would not be able to succeed, he was miserable and didn't know what to do and regretted his actions.

"Sire," she said, "are you dead?"

"Damsel," he said, "not I; but for the rest of the night I shall grant what you have requested of me."

"Sire," she said, "by my faith, if you had granted it when it was requested, you would be better off now."

Gawain was in great anguish, and so was the girl. Neither one slept; instead they lay awake in pain all night until daybreak. As soon as day broke, the host rose quickly and went to the chamber. He did not keep silent or mute, but called out loudly. The damsel quickly opened the door, then lay down nude by him. The knight followed after and saw the two of them lying peacefully and asked them how they were.

Sir Gawain replied, "Sire, quite well, thank you."

When the knight heard him speak so hardily, he was quite unhappy, for it greatly bothered and distressed him.

"What?" he said, "Are you alive?"

"By my faith," said Sir Gawain, "I am quite safe and well. I have done nothing which should cause me to be killed; and if you had harmed or injured me in your house without accusation, it would be wrong."

"What?" he said. "You aren't dead? It greatly annoys me that you are living."

Then he came a little closer and saw the cover which had been cut and the bloody sheets.

"Vassal," he said, "tell me immediately where this blood came from."

Sir Gawain was silent, since he didn't wish to lie, for he didn't know of any explanation with which he could protect himself which the other would not see through.

The host quickly went on. "Vassal," he said, "listen, don't hide anything from me. You wished to do your will on this girl, but you couldn't succeed because of the blade which prevented you."

Sir Gawain said to him, "Sire, you say the truth. The blade wounded me in two places, but not seriously."

When the knight heard that he was not mortally wounded, he said, "Fine sir, you've come out of this well; but tell me—if you wish to escape entirely—your country and your name. You may be of such lineage, fame, and prowess that I should treat you well; but I would like to be certain of it."

"Sire," he said, "My name is Gawain. I am the nephew of good King Arthur. You may be sure of this, for I have never changed my name."

"My faith," said the host, "I know well that you are a fine knight. I couldn't wish to hear of a better one. Your peer doesn't exist from here to Maogre, nor will he be found in all the kingdom of Logre.

"Let me tell you how I have tested every single knight who goes seeking adventures. Each of them was to lie in this bed; and each of them had to die, one by one, until it should happen that the greatest of them all should come. The blade would select him for me, for it would not kill the greatest when he came.

"Now it has happened; it has chosen you as the greatest. Since God has honored you, I wouldn't know how to choose a better man to give my daughter to. I give her to you, pledging that from now on you shall have no harm from me, nor cause for fear; and I promise you in good faith that, for all the days of your life, you shall have the rule of this castle, where you may do what you will."

Gawain thanked him then, joyful and happy. "Sire," he said, "I am well paid with the maiden alone. I do not care for your gold or your silver or this castle."

Then a marriage contract was drawn up between Gawain and the maiden. The news went through the countryside that a knight had come who wanted the maiden and against whom the sword had twice drawn itself without harming him, and they all came quickly.

The castle was filled with the rejoicing of ladies and knights, and the father had rich food prepared. But I don't wish to linger telling what the dishes were. They ate food and drank in plenty. When they had eaten enough and the cloths were removed, the entertainers, of whom there were many, each showed what he knew. One played the viol, another the flute, another the pipes, and others sang or played on the harp or lute. One read romances and another told fables. The knights played at tables, elsewhere, at chess, at mine, or at hasard.

They spent the day in this way until evening, then supped delightfully. There was plenty of fowl and fruits and an abundance of good wine. When they had finished dining joyfully, they went quickly to bed. They took the maiden and Gawain straight to the chamber where they had lain the evening before. The host, who willingly wed them, went with them, then placed the maiden and the knight together safe from danger, then went out and closed the door.

What else can I say? That night he did his will, and no sword was drawn. I am not grieved that he had recovered; it certainly did not grieve the damsel. Sir Gawain remained there in the castle a long time in such joy and revelry; but then he thought how he had stayed for a long time and how his family and friends would surely think that he had been killed. He went to ask his leave of his host. "Sire," he said, "I have remained so long in this land that my friends and my family will think that I have perished. I ask your kind permission to return home; and arrange for this damsel to be prepared so that I, who shall be bringing her, and you, who gave her to me, shall be honored when I return to my country, so they shall say that I have a beautiful love and that she comes from a fine place."

The host gave his leave, and Gawain and the damsel retired. Their palfreys were richly saddled and bridled. The maiden and Gawain mounted their horses. What more should I say? The arms he had borne were brought. He departed upon the farewell of the host, cheerful and happy about his adventure. As they came out of the gateway, the damsel held back on the reins. He asked her why she did so.

"Sire," she said, "I should, for I have forgotten something very important. I would be very reluctant to leave this land without my greyhounds, which I have raised and who are fine and beautiful. You never saw any as swift; and they are whiter than any flower."

Then Gawain turned back, going to get the greyhounds. From out in front the host saw him approaching in the distance. "Gawain," he said, "why are you returning so soon?"

"Sire," he said, "because your daughter forgot her greyhounds, which she tells me she is very fond of; she won't go without them."

The host called them and gave them to him willingly. Gawain returned swiftly with all the greyhounds to the damsel waiting for him. Then they continued on and entered the forest through which he had come.

They saw a knight coming in the path toward them. The knight was traveling alone, but well-armed. He lacked nothing proper to a knight and sat on a bay war-horse, strong, swift, and restless. The knight rode along until he came quite close to them; and Gawain thought to greet him peacefully and inquire who he was and of what land. But the other thought otherwise.

He spurred his horse so fiercely that he charged between the girl and Gawain; without speaking a word, he seized her bridle and turned swiftly back. And she, without anymore request, went unhesitatingly with him. There is no need to ask if Gawain was angered when he saw her thus led off, for he had carried no arms with him except for a shield, a lance, and a sword; and the other, who was well-armed, and large and strong and insolent, had outraged him. Nevertheless, Gawain bravely spurred his horse after him to reclaim the girl.

"Vassal," he said, "you have done a great villainy in seizing my beloved so suddenly. But now act bravely, as I shall describe. You can see very well that I have only my lance and my shield and my sword, hanging at my side. I command you to disarm so that we are equals—this would be the noble thing to do. If you can conquer me through valor, she shall be yours without further dispute.

"If you don't want to do this, then be noble and courteous and wait for me beneath these elms, and I will go borrow arms back there from a friend of mine, and when I am equipped with arms, I will hurry back; and if you can then overcome me, I grant her to you without ill-will. I swear this, truly."

The other immediately replied, "I never asked your permission; and if I've harmed you, I don't ask your pardon. You are very gracious to give me something that's mine, but which you don't want to give up because you are unarmed. Let us resolve it this way: you say that she is your love because she went with you; and I answer that she is mine. Let's put her in this pathway and each draw back. Then let it be entirely up to her which of us she loves the best. If she wishes to go with you, I grant her to you; if she wishes to go with me, then it is right that she should be mine."

Gawain gladly agreed, since he believed in and loved her, for he thought that she surely would not leave him for the whole world. So they left her and each drew back a little. "My dear," they said, "you must decide which one you wish to stay with, for we have left it up to you."

She looked from one to the other, first at him, then at Gawain, who was certain that he would have her and only marveled greatly that she took so long to think about it. But the girl, who knew well what Gawain could do, wanted to know how hardy and valiant the knight was.

Let me tell you, great and small, whether you laugh or whether you groan, that there is hardly a woman alive, whether the mistress or the wife of the best knight from here to India, who would love him or think him worth a pinch of salt if he did not have prowess at home. You know very well what prowess.

Now hear of the great villainy that the girl did. She placed herself in the care of the one she knew nothing of. When Gawain saw this, he was greatly hurt that she should willingly abandon him. But he was so noble and wise, courteous and reasonable, that he didn't say a word, though it grieved him.

The knight said to him, "Sire, the damsel unquestionably ought to be mine."

"God forbid," said Gawain, "that I should question or interfere in something which has nothing to do with me."

Then the girl and the knight rode swiftly off; and Gawain, with all the greyhounds, went off to his own country. But the maiden stopped at the edge of the open land, and the knight asked her why she had. "Sire," she said, "I shall never in my life be your mistress until I have my greyhounds which I see that vassal leading off with him."

And he said to her, "You shall have them." Then he shouted,

"Stop, stop, sir vassal! I order you to halt!" and came rushing up to him. "Vassal," he said, "why are you leading off the greyhounds, when they aren't yours?"

Sir Gawain answered, "Sire, I claim they are mine, and if anyone else claims them, I must defend them as mine. If you wish to play again the game you proposed when we put the damsel in the path to choose which she would stay with, I will gladly agree."

The knight willingly agreed to this, for, like a fool, he thought that if the greyhounds came to him they would remain his without a battle, and he could be certain that if they went to Gawain, he would forcibly lead them off, as he had done before.

They left the road, and when each had gone off, they called; and the dogs went directly to Gawain, whom they knew because they had seen him at the castle of the girl's father. Gawain played with them and talked to them, for he was happy to have them.

But the maiden immediately said to the knight, "Sire, I won't go a single step with you, by God, until I have my dogs, which I love so much."

He answered, "He can hardly lead them off without my permission." Then he said, "Stop this, vassal, for you aren't going to lead them off."

And Gawain said, "It's villainy to go back on your word this way. The greyhounds are mine; they came to me of their own will. May I be deserted by the Lord of Majesty if I ever fail them! I abandoned the damsel, who was mine and came with me, to you only because she went to you. You should rightly leave the greyhounds to me since they are mine, and came with me, and came to me of their own free will.

"And let me tell you one thing for sure; if you want to take your pleasure with this maiden, you'll have brief joy with her. I hope she hears me. You should know how much she was mine, who aided her; and now see how she has served me. Dogs aren't like women, that's for sure. A dog knows one thing: he won't exchange his master who raised him for a stranger. A woman quickly abandons hers if he doesn't do everything she wants. She is so entranced by change that she abandons her own for a stranger. The greyhounds didn't abandon me. This proves undeniably that the nature and love of a dog is worth more than that of a woman."

"Vassal," he said, "your complaint won't do you any good if you don't immediately let them go. Guard yourself; I challenge you."

Gawain seized his shield and thrust it in front of his breast, then rushed upon the other as fast as his horse could bear him, and struck him with such force in the shield beneath the boss that he shattered it, so that the pieces flew as far and as high as the leap of a toad. Then Gawain struck him so mightily in the first quarter of the shield that he threw horse and rider down together into the road.

He fell in the mud between his horse's legs. Gawain drew his steel sword and lifted it against him. He struck down to the earth with it, giving him a great blow on the face and head and stunning him. He put all his strength into it, for he hated him for the malicious deed and the pain he had given him. He greatly injured and hurt him. He lifted the front of his hauberk and struck him with his good sword through the flanks.

When he had avenged himself, he did not look at the horse, nor the hauberk, nor the shield, but went to call the greyhounds, who had loved him so much, and proved themselves to him. Then he ran to catch his horse, which was straying off through the woods, and quickly reached and captured it. He needed no stirrups, but sprang into the saddle.

"Sire," said the damsel, "for the sake of God and for your honor, I beg you not to leave me here, for that would be great villainy. If I was foolish and silly, you shouldn't hold it against me. I didn't dare go with you, I was so frightened when I saw you so poorly furnished with arms, and him so well-armed, lacking nothing."

"My dear," he said, "it's no use. Your explanation is worthless. Such faith, such honor, and such a nature is often found in women. Whoever sows wheat and wishes to reap anything else and he who seeks anything in woman but what is natural to her is not wise. They have been that way since God made the very first one. Whoever strives most to serve them and does them good and honors them, repents most in the end; and the more he honors and serves them, the more he will be angered and the more he will lose.

"Your pity was hardly prompted by concern for my honor and my life; it was prompted by something completely different. As they say, at the end, when everyone has been tested, may God desert whoever has found someone false and yet cherishes and loves and keeps her. Keep your companion."

Then he left her and never knew what became of her. He went on his way, thinking long of his adventure. He wandered through the forest until, at evening, he came to his country. His friends rejoiced, for they had believed he was lost. He told them his adventure from beginning to end. They willingly listened to it—at first, fine and perilous, then ugly and painful—of the love that he lost and then how he fought for the greyhounds with great misfortune. And thus he concluded his tale.

Notes for "The Knight of the Sword"

Le Chevalier à l'epée is the most purely "noble" of all the tales in this collection. It is a short romance, or as Per Nykrog chooses to call it, a lay. The author is conscious of competing with the first great author of Arthurian romances, Chrétien de Troyes. The tale is reminiscent of some of the adventures of Gawain in Chrétien's

Grail romance. All of the separate motifs which make up the tale occur in other romances (see Armstrong, pp. 59–69).

The detailed descriptions of food, clothing, and armor, the motif of the dangerous castle and the dangerous bed, the genteel language both of the narrative and of the dialogue, and of course the very concept of the knight errant in search of adventure, all these belong to the world of courtly romance. This tale was unmistakably destined for the ears of the nobility.

Yet the view of love which the tale presents is quite different from that traditionally associated with the nobility. The moral of the story is that women are inherently faithless, never satisfied with a single lover—a point of view commonly assigned to the bourgeois. It is true that noblewomen are allowed lovers in addition to their husbands, but they are not unfaithful for such light and transient reasons as curiosity about another man's performance in bed. Their motives are of the highest, and no noble romance writer worthy of the name would reproach a princess for taking a lover, so long as she remained faithful to him. (A maiden in the prose *Tristan* behaves as badly as the heroine of this story, but that episode is probably based on "The Knight of the Sword." See Armstrong, pp. 63–64.)

But would her behavior really have surprised or shocked a noble audience? It is instructive to remember that *The Romance of the Rose*, containing some of the most bitterly antifeminist passages in medieval literature, was immensely popular among the nobility. The glorification of women found in many romances does not represent the universal opinion of the aristocracy. There is no reason to suppose that the courtiers residing in a medieval castle were particularly idealistic or high-minded. Although it used to be said that romances and lays were written primarily to please women, I suspect that *jongleurs* may have found an equally eager audience among the male contingent at court, one that possessed an image of feminine nature rather different from that held by the ladies. Such tales as "The Knight of the Sword" would reflect their tastes.

In contrast to the relative refinement of this tale of Gawain's short, unhappy marriage, the one that follows depicts a violent, savage world. But no less than Gawain, its hero is clearly a product of the noble milieu.

The Lady Who Was Castrated

Lords, those of you who have wives who rebel against you and rule over you, you can only bring yourselves shame. Listen to a short example which has been written for you. You may learn from it that you should not do everything your wives desire, so they shall not think less of you. You should punish and admonish foolish ones, so they will not grow proud or try to rule over their lords, but rather cherish, love, obey, and honor them. If they do not, it is to their shame. Now I shall demonstrate in my tale, in the example I shall tell, that those who make their wives the master are dishonored and should listen carefully. What I will tell you is not a bad joke but the truth.

There once was a wealthy man who possessed great riches. He was an honorable knight, but he loved his wife so deeply that she dominated him. He abandoned the rule of his home and lands and gave it to her. But the woman so scorned and despised him that whatever he said, she contradicted and undid whatever he did.

They had a lovely daughter, the fame of whose beauty spread far and wide. Her renown was so widespread that finally a count heard it spoken of. Although he had never seen her, he immediately fell

Source: Anatole de Montaiglon and Gaston Raynaud, eds., *Recueil général et complet des fabliaux des XIIIᵉ et XIVᵉ siècles*, 6 vols. (Paris: Librairie des bibliophiles, 1872–1890), VI: cxlix.

in love with her. If he did love her in this way, it often happens
that one loves without seeing, but only hearing praise. This seems
good. The count had no wife and was young and wise. He was
filled with wisdom worth more to him than any wealth. He said he
would like to see if those who told him about the maiden were
telling the truth or lying. Finally he saw her. Listen to how it
happened:

One day the count went hunting with three knights and a
huntsman leading the dogs. They hunted in the forest until after
nones, when a storm arose. It thundered loudly, lightning flashed,
and it rained heavily. The count's men were separated and lost,
except for the four, who went off together in one direction. The
sun began to set.

The count said, "What is your advice? I don't know what we
can do. We can't reach any of the houses, and the sun is setting. I
don't know where our men are, except that I know they've gone
off somewhere. We must find some shelter, but I don't know what
or where."

While the count was lamenting, they rode down a path into a
garden by a pond belonging to the knight who had the lovely
daughter. They rode along on that unpleasant, rainy day and dismounted beneath an elm. The good man whose house it should
have been was sitting on a stone. The count politely greeted him,
and the other returned his greeting and stood up. The count asked
him for shelter.

"Sire," the knight said, "I would gladly shelter you, for you need
rest. But I don't dare give you shelter."

"You don't dare? Why?"

"Because of my wife, who will never allow anything that I do or
say. She rules over me and governs my house. She is in command
of everything. She doesn't care if I am unhappy. I'm hardly more
than a raincoat to her. She does whatever pleases her, nothing that
pleases me. She won't do anything at my command."

The count laughed at this and said, "If you were brave she wouldn't do this."

"Sire," he said, "so I have learned. But she wants to continue forever this way, unless God has mercy on me. But wait a little here; I'll go down there, and you follow after. Demand shelter rudely, and I'll send you away. If she hears this, I'm certain you'll be well sheltered because I refused you."

They remained and he went off; and when he was inside, they followed him. The count said, "God save your Lordship, and give honor to you and to us."

"Sire Count, God bless you, both you and your company."

But then the count said something else: "Sire, we need shelter: Give us lodging."

"I shall not."

"Why not, Sire?"

"I don't wish to."

"Do so, from good will."

"I tell you I will not, absolutely."

"Out of friendship and for pay, shelter us here until day."

"I would not do it for anything, neither for money nor your prayers."

The lady heard this and jumped up to make her own commands: "Welcome, Sire Count. We'll be happy to receive you. Hurry, dismount."

They dismounted and the servants served them well, as the lady had ordered them to. The lord said, "It is my will that they shall not eat any of my fish or my good venison, or my old wines, or my fruit, or my fowl, or my pastries.

The lady said, "Now make yourselves easy. Don't let his words upset you. In his speech, and in his speech alone, he pretends to be a great lord."

This service was to his liking. The lady took great pains to serve them, seeing that the horses had plenty of oats, because her lord had dared to deny it to them. The lady had a meal quickly readied. There was a great deal of venison and fowls prepared.

Her daughter was in her room, and she didn't want the count to see her, but the lord did. "Lady," he said, "let my daughter be left to eat with your people in the bedchamber and not out here. She is so lovely and has such a noble body, and the count is so young, that if he saw her, he would immediately covet this flower."

The lady said, "But she shall come and eat with us, and he will see her."

The lady dressed her carefully. She was gentle, with lovely coloring. She led her out, and the count took her by the hand and sat her down by him. Her beauty had been highly praised to him, but he found her to be even more beautiful. It seemed to him that she was most lovely. Love struck him in the breast, causing him to love her, so that he wanted to have her as his wife.

Then they washed and were seated. The count, overcome by love, ate with the lovely girl. The cuisine was lavish. They drank many wines and cordials. The count was highly honored. After dining they diverted themselves by talking and had fruit. They washed after the meal in water brought by the squires, then drank some good wine.

The count spoke: "Sire, I ask you to grant me your daughter as my wife. I've never seen anyone lovelier. Give her to me; I want her."

The father said, "You shall not have her. I want to give her to someone of lower rank; that is who I shall give her to."

The lady heard this, jumped up, and said, "Sire, you shall have her. You should know that it isn't up to him to give her away. I give her to you; and with her you shall have silver, gold, and rich clothing. I shall give her to you. Take her."

The count replied, "Thank you. I love her so much that I wish to have her for her beauty and not for wealth. Who has her has not a little."

Then the beds were made up; the three of them went to bed and slept. Love possessed the count. He slept for a while but lay awake longer. Love was advising him what he should do.

When they arose in the morning, they went to the church, taking the maiden with them. The count honored her with money, and the lady offered great wealth, cloth, coins, and boxed drinking vessels. The count said that they had enough. He spoke the truth: "He who takes a good wife gains much; who takes a bad one gains nothing."

The father said, "Daughter, listen to me. If you wish to keep your honor, fear your lord the count. If you do not, it will be to your shame."

The mother said, "I insist you speak with me, dear daughter."

"Gladly, Mother," said the girl.

She spoke into her ear, ordering her: "Dear daughter, keep your head up. Be proud toward your lord. Follow your mother's example, always contradicting your father. He has never said anything that I haven't denied, and I've never done anything he commanded. If you want to have honor, contradict your lord. Thrust him back and push yourself forward, and seldom obey his commands. If you do this, you will be my daughter; if you don't, you will pay for it."

"I will do it if I can," she said, "if I find my lord is lenient enough."

The father could not wait any longer and came forward to beg of his daughter, "My dear daughter, don't believe what your mother says. I beg you to believe me. If you want to have honor, fear your lord, the count, so that no one can speak shamefully of him. Always agree with him. If you don't, you will be wrong and be criticized by everyone."

The count did not want to delay any longer and wished to leave. The rich lord said to him, "Sire Count, I give you my daughter. As a token of my friendship, take this good palfrey and these fine greyhounds, who are bold and hardy and swift."

The count accepted them and thanked him, took his leave, and led his wife off. The count rode along, pondering carefully how and in what way he could make his wife true to him, so that she would not take after her mother, who was so proud and fierce. They entered a field, and one of the greyhounds rushed ahead.

The count said, "Hey, hounds, go ahead! I see you are bold and swift. I command you to catch the rabbit quickly, or you will lose your heads!"

The greyhounds dashed forward but were not able to follow it closely. They turned back, and their lord cut off their heads with his sharp sword.

Then he spoke to his sorrel mare and said, "Don't neigh once more." But the palfrey didn't understand him, and after a little, it neighed again. The count dismounted, cut off its head, and got on another one.

"Sire," said the lady to the count, "you should have cherished this palfrey and those greyhounds for my father's sake, if not for mine. You have killed them, and I don't know why."

The count said, "For one reason: they disobeyed my commands."

The count rode off, leading his wife, thinking up lies, until he came to his largest city. There the barons and sub-vassals were assembled, greatly worried about their lord, for they thought they had lost him. He got down on the bridge and they came forward joyfully to meet him. Some asked him who the lovely woman was.

"Lords, she is your rightful lady."

"Our lady!"

"Yes, my faith! I put the ring on her finger, and she has become my wife."

They joyfully received her. The count prepared for the wedding feast and called his cook to confer with him and order him to make the sauces which he knew pleased him and the highly spiced dishes, "to honor our people and the new lady, so everyone will be joyful together."

The cook said, "I will prepare."

Then the lady spoke with him: "What did the count tell you?"

"To make many good sauces for him."

"Do you wish to please me?"

"Yes, lady."

"Be sure that there isn't a single sauce other than garlic, but make it well."

"I wouldn't dare."

"You will. He won't be angry with you if he knows that I ordered it. You ought to do what I want, for I can help or harm you."

"Lady," he said, "I will do your pleasure, but I hope I won't be shamed! I am your servant in all things."

The cook went off to the kitchen and spent a long time preparing the dishes, using his garlic. After using water, they rose and sat down at the table. The dishes quickly arrived for the lords and all the household; and in every dish there was garlic. But there was also plenty of good wine.

The count was greatly concerned about this. He didn't know what to do and put up with it until the people had dispersed. Then he ordered the cook to come to him in his chamber. He came, but not to his profit. He arrived frightened and trembling.

"Vassal," he said, "by whose order did you use so much garlic and leave out the other seasonings that I ordered you to use?"

When the cook heard this, he didn't know what to do. "Sire," he said, "I'll tell you. I did it because of my lady, Sire, for your lady, Sire, truly. I didn't dare contradict her."

"By the Saints who seek God, you had no permission to disobey my orders!"

The count executed justice on the cook: he pierced him in one eye and tore off an ear and a hand, then exiled him from his lands.

Then he spoke to his companion: "Lady, on whose advice did you do this?"

"On my own, Sire, and I was wrong."

"You did not, by Saint Denis. This was hardly your own idea. Tell me, my love, who gave you this advice?"

"Sire, my mother did, so I would be the same as she; I shouldn't obey your orders, but insist on my own. It would bring me benefits and honor. This time I acted that way, but now, thank God, I repent."

"My dear," said the count, "by God, you shall never be pardoned without punishment!" He leaped forward, seized her by the hair, and flung her to the ground. He beat her with a thorny club until she was almost dead. He carried her unconscious to her bed; and she lay there for three whole months, unable to sit at the table. The count had her well served there until she was healed.

Now you shall hear the result of another example. The gentleman's proud wife desired to see her daughter. She wanted to leave the next day. She readied her knights and went nobly to the court and spoke to her lord as she was used to doing, telling him that he could follow after her if he wanted. He mounted without contradiction, because the lady had told him to, and went after his wife, taking only a squire, who felt little loyalty for him, and a boy on foot, and that was all.

The lady arrived nobly and notified the count that she had come. The count thought she was insane with pride to notify him herself instead of her lord, who he heard had also come. Nevertheless he had fine food and lights prepared.

When the lady was received, it was none too politely, and the count was barely civil to her. Then the father entered, and the count rose to greet him. "Welcome!" he cried out. He ran to help him with the stirrups, and this upset him. The count said, "Sire, allow us to serve you in this house, which is yours, however you wish." He took him by the hand and seated him by him, had him served and his boots removed.

The countess came out of her room with a tender heart for her mother; but she feared the count and remembered him using the club. First she greeted her father, and he her; he kissed her. Then she greeted her mother. She would happily have gone to her, but the count seated her by her father. The mother was unhappy at this.

The cooks hurried to prepare the meal and made a good fire beside the table. They went and sat down to eat. The count greatly honored the lord, sat proudly beside him, and had him nobly served. He had fine dishes and old wines, cordials, and clarets. The proud lady and her company sat at a distance along a bench and were not as well served. The count did this because the woman contradicted her husband in everything. They ate, then had the cloths removed while they diverted and amused themselves. They had some fruit, then went to bed.

Night faded, day appeared. The count rose, sorrowful because the lord had a bad wife. He called him into the hall. "Sire, go hunting in my preserve with dogs, nets, bows and arrows. Go hunt for venison; there's plenty of it. And all the servants and knights will go hunting with you. I'll stay with these ladies, for my head aches. It really pains me."

They mounted and did not delay, but all went hunting. No one remained except the count and four big, proud, strong, powerful servants. He gave his orders to one of his Moors: "Go find the balls of a bull, the balls that hang from his belly. Bring them to me with a knife and a well-sharpened razor. And bring them to me in secret."

He did so without delay.

He took the lady by the arm, sat down by her, and said to her:

"Tell me, God keep you, tell me the answer to what I shall ask you."

"Gladly, Sire, if I know it."

"Where does this pride of yours come from? I would really like to know. What makes you so despise your lord, so that no matter what he says, you say whatever will displease him? How does this happen? A woman can do nothing worse than to hold her lord in contempt."

"Sire, I know more than he does, and he never does anything that pleases me."

"Lady, I know where this comes from. This pride hangs from your loins. I could see it in your eye; you have our sort of pride. You have balls like ours, and that's why your heart is so proud. I would like to feel. If they are there, I'll have them removed."

The lady said, "Silence, good Sire. You shouldn't joke like this with me."

The count couldn't wait. He called his servants and told them: "Quick, stretch her out on the ground. I'll have her loins well searched."

They stretched the lady out, and she cried, "Alas! Misery!" One of the servants took the razor and sliced half a foot into her hip. He thrust his fist in and seemed to pull back and forth on one of the huge bull's balls. She screamed. He pretended to remove it from her body, and put it, bleeding, in a basin.

After this she thought it was real. He began again, and she cried, "Woe! Alas! Curse the day I was born! I'll be smarter from now on. If I can get out of this, I'll never contradict my husband again."

He sliced deep into the other hip and pretended to remove something from her and flung it bleeding into the basin. She suffered so much that she fainted.

When she came out of her faint, the count said, "Lady, now we have your pride that was so bold. Now it will be simple. But I'm afraid some root may remain if I don't cauterize it. Quick, heat me a plowshare to cauterize the roots."

The lady said, "Sire, mercy! I swear to you truly, I'll swear on the saints that I won't contradict my lord. I will serve him as I ought to. I swear to you, on my honor."

"Wait until he returns. Swear to him, and then it will be believed."

"Sire," she said, "I promise."

The countess had a heavy heart and wept long for her mother. The count said to her, "I am happy to have done this to your mother, removing her pride from her. I'm afraid you may take after her and have this pride hanging from your loins. Let me feel; and if I find them, I'll remove them."

"Mercy, Sire, for God's sake! Sire, you ought to know, you've felt there often enough, if they are there. They aren't at all, by God. I am not like my mother, who is stubborn and proud. I take more after my father than my mother, really. I've never disobeyed your orders except once, and I was the worse for it, and you took your vengeance. I assure you, I will do whatever you want and desire. If I don't, you can cut off my head."

The count said, "My dear, I will let this be for now, but if I see that you want to rebel against me, your balls will be removed, just as we have done to your mother. For it is just such testicles that make women proud and foolish."

The noble man returned from hunting, having killed a great deal of venison. He heard the lady crying and hurried to ask what was wrong with her. The count met him and said, "Sire, I've removed what caused her to be so proud. She had these two balls at her loins, which made her a proud woman. Here are the balls in this basin. There was no other way to stop it. I wanted to cauterize the roots, but she wanted to swear by the saints that she would never contradict you and always willingly serve you. After she has sworn, if she begins to scorn you again, just open the wounds with hot irons and cauterize the roots and nerves."

The other thought this was all true, since he saw the balls there; and he thought that the wounded lady was improved. The lady swore her oath and promised, without delay. They had her wounds bound up, a litter prepared, and the two horses carried her off. Her wounds were not mortal. She had a good doctor who healed her completely. She loved and served her lord and never again contradicted him in anything.

The count did well. Blessed be he, and blessed are those who punish their evil wives. The other was shamed, as are those who are ruled by their wives. You should love, honor, and greatly cherish the good ones, and consider evil, contrary ones as quarrelsome whores. This is the ending of this fabliau: Damn the woman who despises a man!

Notes to "The Lady Who Was Castrated"

The theme of castration is fairly common in fabliaux (see "The Lay of Ignaurés" and "Aloul"). In *La Dame escoillée* the theme is presented in almost Freudian purity. While the count's diagnosis of the disdainful lady's ailment as testicular envy deserves a place in the annals of psychoanalysis, the insanely savage cruelty of the count himself is also worthy of scrutiny. He is a biologically oriented Petruchio, a first-rate shrew-tamer; yet his cooly barbaric dismembering of the hapless cook and his treatment of the mother and daughter smack more than a little of the Marquis de Sade.

Surely this strange tale does not qualify as a courtly romance. It is commonly regarded as a fabliau, however, and it is printed in all the standard fabliaux collections and accepted as such by Nykrog. He even considers it a "classic" fabliau, since it is contained in no less than five manuscripts. Yet the milieu is distinctly noble, the author addresses himself to lords embroiled in marital difficulties, and many of the descriptions and much of the terminology belong to the courtly style.

But we are confronted with the author's fondness for extremely blunt language and uncourtly turns of phrase, his rather crude sense of humor, and his emphasis on physical details. It is clear that such a tale is in no way foreign to the spirit of the medieval court. The tale is a vigorous, infuriated reassertion of the traditional male dominance of women in the face of the growing cult of courtly love.

The *jongleur* must have often found himself caught between masculine and feminine points of view, if—as I suspect—the ladies delighted in tales of genteel adultery, the men, in stories of savage revenge. Perhaps the next tale, "The Lay of Ignaurés," was composed as a compromise, an attempt to please both sides. If so, the author must have succeeded admirably.

The Lay of Ignaurés*

RENAUT DE BEAUJEU

He who loves should never hide it; rather he should tell of it in fitting words so others may learn and follow a good example. He may receive blessings and honor, though he will not thereby gain wealth. People no longer understand about knowledge and wisdom or about silver and gold. Gifts are taken away; no one receives recompense any more. Wisdom is lost and hidden. To whomever it is revealed and shown, he should spread it everywhere.

Therefore, I would like to tell of a strange adventure which happened at one time in Bretaigne, to a knight of great prowess who should be remembered. The knight's name was Ignaurés, and he was of great renown. He was born in the land of Hoel at the noble castle of Riol. He achieved so much by his prowess that there was not another knight as worthy in the land.

There never was and never will be a happier man. When it was just the beginning of May, he rose at dawn, taking with him five *jongleurs,* flute players, and pipers. The young man went out to the woods, noisily bringing in May. Ignaurés used to disport this way every day.

Source: Renaut de Beaujeu, *Le Lai d'Ignaure ou Lai du prisonnier,* ed. Rita Lejeune. Académie royale de langue et littérature françaises de Belgique. Textes anciens, 3 (Bruxelles: Palais des académies, 1938).
* The name means "he of whom others are ignorant."

He was possessed and inflamed by noble love ~~for a woman~~ *and the women*
~~named~~ *called him* Lousignol. There were twelve peers belonging to the court
in the castle at Riol. They were bold and wise men, rich in lands
and income. Each one had a lovely, noble wife, born of high
lineage, from a great family. Ignaurés, who had a noble heart,
came to know all of them and promised each of them his love. He
said that whatever they wished of him, he would serve them as if
he were a count. Each one thought he was hers, which made them
happy and pleasant. When he came to each one, he forgot all the
others and didn't even remember that he had desired them. He
led a very courteous life.

When a tournament was held, he went to gain prizes from
twenty or even thirty knights. He had little income, but he astonished everyone because the ladies gave him so much that he was
able to rejoice. Ignaurés was quite a young man!

He loved them all for more than a year, when it came time for
the feast of Saint John, which delights all living creatures.* It
happened that all twelve of the noble ladies went to amuse themselves in a garden orchard. There was no one there except the
twelve of them. There was one of them who was very eager to say
what she was thinking (and damn whoever tried to stop her from
saying what she wanted!).

"I know you would give me permission to tell you something if
you knew the reason behind it."

"Say what you are thinking. We will all let you."

"We are ladies, happy, lovely, noble, and worthy. We are the
wives of the peers of this castle, and we are filled with delight.
Every one of us is in love, and this is a joyful day. Let us make one
of us a priest. She shall sit here in the center by this flowering tree.
Each of us will see her and tell her, as in confession, whom she
loves. She shall give one of us the prize, and thus we shall know
which of us loves most nobly."

* The feast of Saint John the Baptist falls on June 24.

All of them replied, "That's well said. We agree without dissent. You yourself shall be the priest and hear the confessions. Go sit down beside the tree."

"I agree," the gentle lady said.

One of them, clothed in a rich tunic and a gray mantle, rose, came to the priest, and laughed.

"What do you seek?" the master said.

"I come to confess, Sire Priest."

"Then sit down and tell me—and be careful not to lie—the name of your lover."

"He is the knight of greatest renown in this whole empire. Do you know who I mean? You know him, the most handsome one. Ignaurés, the bold, the wise—he's the one to whom I've given myself."

The priest blushed when she heard her lover named (she was the one who loved him most). She could barely control herself: "Lady, allow the others to come. I have heard what you had to say."

Another came up, beating her breast with her right hand. "Sweet sister, do not beat your breast any more. Who made you commit the sins with which your body is stained?"

"Sire, I come to repent."

"I order you in penitance to name me your lover, lovely friend."

"Certainly. I shall not lie. I can name you the most courteous man from here to Vermandois, the most handsome and the wisest."

"You value him highly. I do not know if the evidence will support you."

"My faith! You misjudge him. His name is Ignaurés, the noble."

When the priest heard the one she thought pledged to her named again, her blood boiled. "Lady, go and sit down."

A lovely, valiant, joyful lady then came forward. "Sit down, wise lady." She made her sit, then ordered her to tell the name of her lover, insisting that she tell the truth.

"He who is the best, the most courteous, the most dutiful, who has nothing to do with outrages. You shall know the name of the one to whom I have completely given myself. He really should be a king or a count. I can name him, for he is the gentlest. His name is Ignaurés, the flower of nobility."

When the priest heard her, her blood rushed away and her face grew pale. "Lady, now go back and sit down. You have a handsome and noble lover."

Dressed regally in cloth from Constantinople, another came courteously forward. She had a ring on her finger. As she heard birds singing in the tree, she kissed and stroked the ring. "Lady," said the priest, "sit down. I believe you don't hate the one whose ring that was!"

She replied, "He should be a count!"

"Then name him, since he is so noble."

"It is Ignaurés, the flower of nobility." When she heard this, she almost went out of her mind. But she controlled her expression. "Now lady, go back and sit down."

Then a lovely, very polite lady came forward. "Tell me, lady, the name of the one who has the gift of your heart."

"The land resounds with his name. People call out his name when it thunders to protect themselves, so lightning will not strike them."

"You're wrong," said the priest. "You've often said his name, but that didn't prevent a certain bolt from striking you! His name will never save you or deflect those lightning bolts."

"May God bring such blows back to me! I don't complain of their number."

"Lady, let us leave this, and name me his name, sweet sister."

"He is Ignaurés of the noble heart, before whom all Bretaigne trembles." The lady smiled against her will, marveling that this man was named by each of the ladies. They recalled no one else.

When they had all confessed, they came together to the priest: "Lady, tell us who it seems to you has the most valiant lover?"

"To tell the truth, each one has told me the name of the same, single knight. He has greatly disgraced us. I love him as well, just as all of you do! By God! This is an evil deed! Ignaurés has condemned himself. He will pay for it without delay.

"How can we avenge ourselves?"

They all promised that she to whom he came first would grant him a rendezvous in the orchard, along with all of them, without fail. "She will let us know the day, and we will all be there. Everyone bring a sharp knife! We will take cruel vengeance for his mad audacity and malice."

They all agreed to this and went away, out of the garden, each with pain in her heart.

Ignaurés, who knew nothing of this plot, went to one of them. He kissed and embraced her, but could not go further with her. "Lady, how does it happen that you act like a stranger to me?"

"Sire, I am not acting like a stranger. I must control myself for now; but I want you to promise to come and speak with me Sunday in my lady Climenche's orchard. There you can do your will."

"Lady," he said, "at your pleasure. I shall obey your commands." He quickly took his leave. Then the noble man was sentenced to death; unless he discovered what was going on, or fortune kept him from returning.

She had the others warned, and on Sunday they hid themselves in the orchard, well provided with good knives which they kept under their mantles. She who was betraying him came nobly into the orchard, so Ignaurés would see his love there. He came by another path. He had a servant with him who carried all the messages and took charge of his income.

The waiting lady had left the gate open, and the brave man went straight in. He would suffer before going out again. The lady came up to him, and he sent his messenger back home. He didn't care to have him watch him. She closed and locked the gate, softly and quietly; and they went and sat down under a tree. The young man embraced the lady and gently kissed her. She didn't want to allow him anything else, for he was seized by desire.

The ladies who had loved the handsome, happy knight rushed out from all sides, inflamed with anger and rage.

"Ladies," he said, "is this an ambush? You've caught me in your trap."

They went to the seat and gathered in a circle. Ignaurés spoke to them. He said, "You are welcome!"

"But you," they said, "are ill come. You must pay for your outrages. Before you leave this place you will get the reward of a false man, a disloyal man, a traitor."

The priestess spoke first: "Please, I beg you, allow me to .say what I want. Then each of you can say what she wants. Ignaurés, do not lie to me. I have been your love for many days. I gave my heart to you."

"Lady, I am your love, your man, and your knight with all my heart and soul."

One of them disdainfully rose and spoke to him proudly: "Ignaurés, you are a wretch! What? Aren't you my lover?"

"Yes lady, may God save me. I have never failed to love you from my heart, nor ever shall, so long as I live."

Another was envious and looked at him cruelly: "Ah! Evil traitor! You don't say that to me! So, do you love someone other than me? You are pledged to be mine."

"Lady, I love you, truly, and will love you. I'll never deny it."

"What?" said another. "What are you saying? Didn't you promise to love me?"

"Yes, with all my strength, both you and all the others. I love you all, have no doubts; I love their solace and their delight."

Then you could hear a great noise of women fighting and quarrelling, threatening the good vassal. They pulled out the knives which they had hidden. "Ignaurés, you have sinned so much that you must surely die. No one can save you except God."

"Ladies, don't be so cruel to commit such a great sin. If my helmet were laced on and I were on a war horse from Aquilée with a shield at my neck and a lance in my hand, I would dismount here and put myself at your mercy. If I die at such lovely hands, I shall be a martyr with the saints! Now I know I was blessed at my birth."

When they heard this, they all wept. This fine speech by the knight had greatly softened them. She who had heard the confessions said, "Ladies, if you please, grant that we do as I wish."

"We grant it, since it pleases you."

"Ignaurés, you deceived us well until we discovered it. We shall not love you any more at all, for we remember this. Let the one who pleases you most be yours and remain yours. Each one wants her own love."

"I wouldn't do that for anything. I will still love you all, just as I have done up to now."

"Obey my command," said the priest, "or you will die now, by my head! Take the one of us you want."

"Lady," he said, "it is you. I am sad at my loss, for they are all very worthy; but your love is dear to me."

"Thank you very much," the gentle lady said.

The others were very unhappy, but they nevertheless swore that they would not love him any more and would leave him in peace. When things had been thus settled, they all went home again, and Ignaurés returned to the town.

Now he went often to his mistress. If he had still had all of them, he would have seldom gone to her; but now he had only one path to tread. He went often, not caring who saw him. In fact, through going too often, he was betrayed and lost. The mouse that has only one hole is soon caught. In some way or other what the foolish women had told each other in confession when they were sitting in the orchard got out.

There was a false and cruel liar in the castle. She who was trying to hide her actions often went there, and he eventually discovered what she was doing. Once he knew, he didn't hide it. One day the twelve peers all went to eat together. The knave went with them, and before they left the house, told them a tale which made even the happiest of them angry. The traitor began to speak, laughed, and crossed his head.

"What are you laughing at, knave? This is a poor hors d'oeuvre. I know what you're up to. Nobody should mock our dishes."

"My faith," he said, "I know a marvel which I can hardly tell you. I can't keep from laughing."

"God keep you! Is it something about us?"

"Yes, by God. It's about all of you."

"Tell the truth. We're ready."

"I would, if I got something for it."

"You'll get something, don't be afraid."

"If I had a pledge from you, I would tell you, by Saint Germain!"

One of them said, "I will guarantee your safety."

"Lords, if I tell you the truth about an affair—about which I am absolutely certain—will you do me no harm or injury?"

"Not at all. We won't say a word against you."

"You are all cuckolds, by a single man! I swear as I see you here. He is a lord and master."

When they heard this, they trembled with rage at this evil villain.

"Is he a bourgeois or a knight? What is his name?"

"It's been well hidden. The vassal's name is Ignaurés, who sins against what is right." He told them the whole adventure of the confessions in the orchard and how the infuriated women wanted to stab him with their knives. "Then the young man was terrified, because he was close to death. They told him to choose the one who pleased him best, and she remained alone with him while the others went away. They would never love him again, whether he wanted them to or not. He chose one of your wives, the most beautiful and the wisest. I know which one it is that rules the others."

"Which one is it? Do you know?"

He said to one of them, "It's yours!"

The other replied, infuriated, "By God! If I was sure of that I'd be more worthy than the others."

When the meal was over they made him swear not to tell anyone else about this affair. They gave him his reward and sent him on his way. The others remained, lamenting their shame to each other. "We must rule this castle. If we can't avenge ourselves, then we're sorry wretches."

Said one, "I agree. If you will follow my plan we will have full vengeance. There is no use setting spies since he has abandoned them all except the one he goes to often. If her husband will promise to watch where he goes, we can easily catch him."

"That's well said," they all agreed. The other, trembling with rage, said he certainly would watch for him.

"Sire, let us know when you have taken him. We will all come and avenge ourselves of our shame." To this they all agreed.

They returned to their homes, anxious to punish the guilty one. He, who was quite happy, was enjoying himself in the castle near his mortal enemies. The one whose wife was his mistress spied on him day and night, to trap him. If he could surprise him with his wife, all the others would fulfill their pledge. Ignaurés went too often to enjoy himself with his mistress. But the mouse that has only one hole is soon trapped and taken.

He was surprised one morning lying with the lady. The lord who knew all about them discovered it through a spy of his. He entered the stone-walled chamber from a subterranean vault with his helmet laced on and his sword drawn. He found Ignaurés, suspecting nothing, making love to his wife.

"Aha!" he said. "You have no business here!"

"Sire," he said, "for God's sake, mercy! You see how it is. I have sinned against you. I can't deny or conceal it."

The lord had two bachelors with him, his nephews. They wanted to cut Ignaurés up, but the lord told them not to. They would have a better revenge. "You shall not kill him, by my soul!"

The lord spoke to his wife: "Lady, you must bathe your lover, and then you will have him bled. Be sure your lord has white sheets."

The lady tore her hair, filled with anguish. Then the lord led the vassal off and had him secretly guarded in a stone-floored chamber by people he trusted. He swore to bring him pain and shame. His dinner would be poor indeed. Then he had the other peers informed of what he had done.

The lady was in great torment; and she had the other ladies informed of all that had befallen her, how she had been surprised with Ignaurés: "I don't even know if he is dead or alive! All of you had what you wanted from him. Lament with me. Just as we all had joy together, let us share our common grief."

They all promised to the messenger that they would not eat again until they knew for sure if he were alive or dead. Then they began to fast.

Meanwhile the lord had all of his companions gather secretly. They took counsel together to decide what sentence they could impose on him who caused them shame and dishonor. One said, "Those filthy whores have all sworn to fast until they know whether he is dead or will escape. On the fourth day, let us remove from the vassal that low member whose delight used to please them. We'll make them eat it, along with his heart. We'll prepare two dishes and get them to eat by a trick. There is no better way to avenge ourselves."

They agreed to this plan, and dismembered the good knight. As they had agreed before, they prepared the dishes and served them to the fasting ladies. Each of them was eased in her heart when she had swallowed down that fine and savory dish. Their lords lied to them to make them eat and drink, and they did not disdain it. When their spirits had returned, they begged their lords to tell them, for the love of God, if he was free from prison.

The one who had caught him in his house replied, "Lady priestess, you used to be his mistress. You have eaten your great desire, that which gave you so much pleasure; for you wanted nothing else. Finally you are justly served! I killed your lover, and you have all shared in the delight of that part which women are most greedy for. Have you had enough? Now we're avenged of our shame!"

The lady immediately fainted, and on reviving, she began to sigh and weep. She hated death for delaying to take her and cared for nothing in the world. She sent to her companions and informed them about the dish which they had boldly eaten. They all made a vow to God that they would never eat again, no matter what fine dishes they had. Thus they spoke, and thus they did.

While they lived, they all lamented. One lamented his beauty, his handsome, soft limbs, and how they had destroyed his most lovely member. Thus they spoke of the young man. Two others lamented his great courage, his noble body, and his generosity. The fourth lamented his flanks and his gray and laughing eyes. Another lamented his sweet heart. There would never be such another worthy one.

"Alas! How we have changed you. Those jealous men avenged themselves too cruelly! But we will not eat; in this way we will avenge ourselves."

Another lamented his fine feet which sat so nicely in the stirrups. He was more skilled at hunting with hounds and hawks than anyone—and delightful. Each one lamented the loss of her pleasure with him, who was so good with them in bed. Everyone who heard their laments wept for them. The gentle ladies would not eat, neither for the sake of their friends or their families. They could not forget their lover. They went mad, wringing their hands, sighing, and crying their laments.

The twelve of them mourned together. The lay, which should

be remembered, has twelve verses. The story is completely true. Renaut is a witness to this: Ignaurés, the good vassal, died. Those who were his mistresses died for love of him. May God have mercy on their souls, both on the ladies and the knights.

And blessed be he who made this lay, which should please lovers. She has bound me fast, so I can never be released. She has a long, white neck with no bone or wrinkle to be seen. She is simple and polite and whiter than new-fallen snow. You shall not have any more open description of her; the other parts are covered. This is the best part when bound by love's chains. But I don't want to be one of those who thinks he can say the truth about it, except I can see her little breasts raise up her tunic from underneath. They raise it so high that they seem to be quite firm. She has lovely shoulders, slender hands and fingers, lovely arms in her sleeves. She is slightly broad in the hips and narrow in the waist. She is beautifully shaped, not too small nor too large. She is marvelously well-formed and has fine manners. She is love's chain itself! This lady can lead me wherever she wants by her chain. I am in a sweet prison and have no desire to escape through ransom.

That is the story of the lay which I now finish for you here. Frenchmen, Poitevins, and Bretons call it "The Lay of the Prisoner." It was written for Ignaurés, who was dismembered for love.

Notes to "The Lay of Ignaurés"

Around the beginning of the thirteenth century, Renaut de Beaujeu wrote his gaily gory *Lai d'Ignaurés*. As opposed to the horror attached to cannibalism in classical mythology, Renaut thinks it's funny. Of all the many versions of the "eaten heart" theme (see pp. 28–29 in Lejeune), this is the only humorous one—medieval black humor.

Again, there can be no question that the tale was meant for a noble audience. The first half of the story comprises a perfectly orthodox lay, delicate and sentimental, if lightly comic, deeply concerned with human emotions; and the second half is a strange mixture of the macabre and the genteel. But the whole is pervaded by Renaut's urbane and witty spirit, and he shows no sign whatever of thinking his tale in any way unsuited for aristocratic ears. (The manuscript in which it is preserved contains both fabliaux and lais.)

He even concludes, rather unexpectedly, with a rapturous description of his lady. The lay was evidently written for her, as other writers dedicated their writings to their own ladies. But even here Renaut cannot keep his spirit in the narrow bounds of convention. His description is a mixture of courtly love commonplaces and vulgar confidences about the lady's body. Love or death, the lighthearted Renaut simply refuses to take anything seriously. John Benton has suggested that perhaps Renaut's beloved was in the audience and that guessing her identity would be a game for the audience like that played by the ladies in the story.

The next tale is written by the very serious Marie de France, whose gravity is quite as capable of assimilating horrors as is Renaut's cheerfulness.

Equitan

MARIE DE FRANCE

There have been many noble Breton lords of Britain. In former times they used to make lays to recall and prevent from being forgotten their nobility, their courtesy, and the adventures which they had heard of happening to many people. They made one which I have heard which is not to be forgotten of Equitan, who was the courteous ruler, king, and lord of Nantes.

Equitan was very worthy and greatly beloved in his land. He loved the pleasures of courtship; and for this reason he upheld knighthood. Those who know nothing of love care nothing about their lives. This is the measure of love: it should make one abandon reason. Equitan had a seneschal, a good knight, virtuous and loyal. He cared for, maintained, and ruled over all his lands; for the king himself would not abandon his hunting, his pleasures, or his sports by the river, unless he had to wage war because of some emergency which had arisen. The seneschal had a wife to whom great evil came later in that land. The lady was marvelously beautiful and well adorned with a lovely form, a noble body. Nature took pains in fashioning her. She had gray eyes and a pretty face, a lovely mouth, none better placed. Her peer did not exist in the entire realm.

The king had heard her often praised, and he himself often

Source: Marie de France, *Lais*, ed. Alfred Ewert (Oxford: Basil Blackwell, 1963), pp. 26–34.

saluted her. He sent her some of his belongings; he desired her when he could not see her and spoke with her as often as he could. He went off into the country to hunt and enjoy himself in private. The king lodged one night, returning from his sport, in the castle which the seneschal ruled, where the lady was. There he was able to speak with her at length and show her his feelings and desires. He found her courteous and wise, with a lovely face and body, cheerful and friendly. Love had him in his power. He had shot an arrow at him, making a large wound, aiming it so that it struck his heart. There was no need for sense or understanding, for he had so overwhelmed the lady that it made her sad and pensive. She had to listen to it all and could not defend herself.

That night he did not rest or sleep but blamed and accused himself. "Alas," he said, "what destiny led me into this country? Seeing this lady has struck me with anguish in my heart; my whole body trembles. I think she must love me; but if I love her, I will do wrong. She is the seneschal's wife. I ought to keep my faith with him and my love for him, just as I would like him to do for me. I know that if he found out about this in any way it would greatly grieve him.

"Nevertheless, it would be worse to be frightened off by him. It would be too bad if such a lovely lady never loved nor had a lover! What will become of her courtesy if she does not engage in love? There is not a man beneath Heaven who would not be improved by her love. From what I've heard, I shouldn't worry too much about the seneschal. He cannot keep her to himself. I am determined he shall share her with me."

When he had said this, he sighed and lay there thinking. Then he spoke, saying, "Why am I distressed and suffering? I don't even know yet if she will take me as her lover, but I will know soon. If she feels as I do, then I shall escape this suffering. Ah, God! How long it is until morning! I cannot get any rest. It has been a long time since I went to bed last night."

The king watched until it was day, waiting in pain. He arose and went hunting, but he soon turned back, saying to himself that he was very unhappy. He went to his room and lay down. (The seneschal was unhappy because he didn't know what was causing the king to suffer so; but his wife was the direct cause.) To divert and comfort himself, he sent for her to come and speak with him. He revealed his feelings to her and made her realize that he was dying for her. She could completely comfort him, or else she could cause his death.

"Sire," the lady told him, "I must have time. Just now I don't know what I should do. You are a king of great nobility. I am not so exalted that you should choose me for romance or love. If I did your will, I know without a doubt you would soon abandon me, and I would be greatly injured. If I did love you and granted you your request, this love would not be evenly shared between the two of us, for you are a powerful king and my lord is your vassal. I think you believe you have the right to love as a *seigneur*. But love is not good if it is not equal. A poor but loyal man, if he is wise and worthy, is better and brings more joy in love than a prince or king who lacks loyalty. If someone loves more highly than suits his position, he is afraid of everything; and on his side, the nobleman thinks that nothing can rob him of his beloved. He wants love by means of his lordship."

Equitan then replied, "Thank you, lady. Say no more! This is hardly fine, courteous talk. This is bourgeois bargaining, for those who concern themselves with unworthy objects for wealth and fiefs. There is no woman under Heaven, if she is wise, courteous, and noble, even if she has nothing but her mantle, provided that she honors love and is not fickle, who does not deserve that the powerful prince of a castle should labor for her and love her loyally and well. Those who are inconstant in love and take pains to deceive are themselves deceived and fooled. We have seen many cases of this. It is no marvel if one gets what he deserves for his labors. My beloved lady, I surrender myself to you! Do not consider me as a king, but as your man and your lover! I swear to you truly that I will do your pleasure. Don't let me die because of you. You shall be the mistress, and I shall be the servant; you proud, and I submissive."

The king spoke with her and begged her mercy until she assured him of her love and granted him her body. They held each other by their rings and pledged their faith to each other. They kept faith well and loved each other deeply. This would cause their death, their end.

Their love endured a long time unknown to others. When they came together and wanted to talk, the king had his people told that he was having himself bled in private. The doors of the chambers were shut, and no man could be found so bold as to enter them unless the king had sent for him.

The seneschal sat in the court, hearing pleas and accusations. The king loved her for a long time and cared for no other woman. He did not want to marry anyone, nor would he hear talk of it. The people thought him at fault, and the seneschal's wife heard of this. It grieved her, and she was afraid of losing him. When she could speak with him, and he wanted to enjoy himself with her—kiss, embrace, caress, and lie with her—she wept bitterly and showed her great sorrow. The king asked and inquired what this could be; and the lady answered: "Sire, I am weeping for our love, which is causing me great anguish. You will take a wife, a king's daughter, and separate from me. I've often heard it said, and I know it's true. And I, alas! What will be come of me? I must die because of you, for I know no other comfort."

The king said, filled with love, "My dearest love, don't be afraid! Certainly I will never take a wife or desert you for another. Know this and believe it: if your husband were dead, I would make you my wife and queen. I will not abandon you for anyone."

The lady thanked him and said it greatly rejoiced her to have him assure her that he would not leave her for anyone else. She would quickly arrange for her lord's death; for it would be easy to arrange if he wished to aid her. He replied that he would do so. Whatever she proposed, whether for good or evil, he would undertake to do.

"Sire," she said, "if it pleases you, go hunting in the forest in the land where I live, and stay in my lord's castle. There you will be bled, and on the third day, bathed. My husband will be bled and bathed with you. Order him to; don't let him escape. He must keep you company. I will have the baths heated and carried in two tubs. His bath will be so boiling hot that no man alive beneath Heaven would escape being scalded and hurt if he sat in it. When he is scalded and dead, you shall call in your men and his and show them how he died suddenly in his bath."

The king agreed to everything; he would do her will. Within three months the king went hunting in that country. He had himself bled, along with his seneschal, to prevent illness. On the third day he said he would bathe, and the seneschal was quite willing.

"You shall bathe with me," he said.

The seneschal answered, "I agree."

The lady heated the bath water and had the two tubs carried in. She placed the tubs before each of the beds as planned. She had the boiling water carried where the seneschal was to bathe. The good man got up and went out to divert himself. The lady sat down by the king to talk with him. They lay on the lord's bed and amused themselves and enjoyed each other. They lay there together, by the tubs. They had the door watched and guarded by a maidservant standing there.

The seneschal suddenly returned and pushed the door, but she held it against him. He struck it so angrily that he forced it open. There he found the king and his wife lying in each other's embrace. The king looked up and saw him coming; and, to cover his villainy, he jumped heedlessly with both feet, naked and bare, into the tub. There he was scalded and died. His evil returned to him, and the other was safe and well. The seneschal saw clearly what had happened to the king. He seized his wife and put her in the bath head first. Thus they both died: first the king, then she with him.

Whoever can understand reason may grasp the meaning of this example: whoever plots harm to others, that harm returns to him. It happened just as I have told you here. The Bretons made a lay of it, called *Equitan*, how he died and with him the lady he loved so dearly.

Notes to "Equitan"

In the last third of the twelfth century Marie de France wrote her famous lays, which she claimed were Welsh stories retold in French verse and which contributed importantly to the Celtic influence on continental literature. Marie's claims to nobility were impeccable, and she was familiar with royalty, especially in Norman England, where she lived and wrote. Of all courtly writers, she is perhaps the most deeply concerned with shades of emotion and delicate questions of morality and propriety.

Even in *Equitan* these fundamental concerns are apparent. Nothing is more typical of her style than the nocturnal musings of the lovesick king or the guarded reasoning of the lady. The basic spirit of the tale, however, is far removed from these concerns. It has been called vulgar and sordid, as if the inevitable comparison were to a hatchet murder described in a common tabloid; but we might as well say that the story illustrated what would have happened if Agamemnon had turned the tables on Clytemnestra.

Yet we must admit that in the context of medieval literature, the husband's wrathful revenge and the author's seeming sympathy with him are far more typical of the fabliau than of the average lay. (Many husbands are successfully duped in the fabliaux, of course; but such incidents are usually meant to satirize women's perverse ingenuity, not to support their faithlessness.) If the husband does triumph in other lays, it is seen as a tragedy. Here he seems to be justified, and his wife is portrayed in sharp contrast to the usual lady of romance. There is no question that something of the fabliau spirit penetrated even the quintessentially courtly world of Marie de France.

Audigier

Some tell of Audigier who know nothing about him, but I will tell you about him until you cry, "Enough!" His father ruled Cuckoldland, a soft country where the people are in shit up to their elbow. I got there by swimming through a stream of crap, and I couldn't get out again through any other hole.

Audigier's father was from Cuckoldland; he was the son of Turgibus, the son of Poitruce. When this fellow stretched out and shook himself, his heart swelled like a flea. He had a thin neck, as long as an ostrich's. When he shit all over his clothes, he stuck his fingers in the crap and sucked on them; then nothing bothered him. When the call to arms was given, he hid himself.

You shall now hear the life of Count Turgibus. He loved nothing so well as gruel and goat with sorb-apples* at splendid feasts, for he was raised in Lombardy where they treat them as great dainties. When the bold fellow began his chivalry, he cut a thistle stalk with his sword, so he could have it scratching his breast. He had a yellow, pale, puffy face. There wasn't such a handsome knight from here to Jachie (that's a land where God isn't at all).

Source: Omer Jodogne, ed., "*Audigier* et la chanson de geste, avec une édition nouvelle du poème," *Le Moyen âge*, ser. 4, vol. 15 (1960), pp. 495–526.
    * *Sorbus domestica*, related to both the apple and the pear.

Count Turgibus' valor was great. When he came through chivalry to France, he showed his virtue and strength; he thrust his lance through a cobweb. But, by mischance, a tree stump struck him, and his horse threw him under its belly. When the fellow saw that he was not strong enough, he paid the stump proper homage and kissed it three times to remember it. Thus peace was made and an alliance formed.

Count Turgibus was of great renown. One day he took his bow and his great arrow and, aiming well, made a fine shot. He placed the arrow, stretching it back to the feather, in his bow (which was stiffer than a reed). With one shot he pierced the wing of a butterfly which he found perched by a bush, and after that, it could hardly fly, if at all.

Rainberge, who at this time still had no husband, came out of her house. She turned around, bent over, and showed him everything, cunt and asshole. "Come forward," she said, "son of a baron; squat down with me and we'll shit together. Yesterday I ate an abundance of prunes, and the pits are shooting out of my ass. I didn't bring a rag to wipe myself. Polish my ass with your shirttail, or else you shall not have the gift of my love."

"Lady," said the fellow, "we shall do so. We should never lose your love through failing to perform such a service." Then he polished her ass all over, and, with drinking cups, they were engaged.

Lady Rainberge was intelligent and wise. She was never tired of shitting well. Turgibus watched her with desire, for there was not so beautiful a girl in the land. Because she squinted a little and was mangy and because he saw she was so much in love, and gave such juicy, drooling kisses with her mouth, behold Father Renier marrying them. Rainberge brought him a handful of dung, then took some of her piss and sprinkled him with it. "That's as good for you, sir priest, as a cupping."

Then Turgibus had a fine mate; when he drew near her he found her as soft as a shell. He gave her fifteen dog turds as a dowry. Then the gracious lady thought of herself; she let four farts in his face. "Look, sire," she said, "see if it smells. I'm storing plenty of it for you in this locker. Tomorrow you should hold a great feast. Be careful to be gracious and wise."

Turgibus held the wedding feast by a swamp, and the lords of Cuckoldland came, packing up all their harness in a basket. They spread out the cloths on seven stumps and ate fresh cheese. Then they had another dish: four baked rats for dessert. "Ah, God!" said Turgibus, "what a dessert! If only we had something to drink afterward!"

"Drink away, sire," said Rainberge, "I'm coming. You'll have plenty to drink with all your dishes, for I've got a bellyful of foul wind."

After the dishes I've told you of, they had four old roasted crows dipped in cowflops. Because of this the dish was so fine that it stank. "Ah, God," said Turgibus, "how well we are served. Now if we only had something to drink, we would be well off."

"Then drink," said Rainberge, "what I have here." The lady held him and the count held her. "Luckily," said the lady, "I'm not shitting, for last night I had too much boiled milk."

That night Audigier was engendered, who was of strong, hardy lineage and the most craven of cowards.

Turgibus was killed by an accident. He had gone to disport himself in a ditch, but at nightfall bats assailed him, beetles assailed him on a dungheap, and flies came to leave droppings on him, until he could no longer rise, and he let himself fall onto the dungheap. His soul issued out through his rear, and his body performed miracles that night. Everything came there to rot; even the dogs of the land went there to piss, thinking they could cure his madness.

At that time Rainberge was pregnant, ready to give birth, so that she couldn't wipe her ass. When she was delivered of the devil, the lady began to celebrate.

When Audigier was born, there was joy. The lady lay by an

elder tree where sows and hogs had lain, for the warmth of the dung which she felt. Her companion there was Lady Poitru. All the noble peers came there: Aubree and Coquelorde and Ermentru. The best dressed of them were clothed in old sacking. They had a vulture which they had taken with birdlime and with which they stuffed themselves nicely that evening. They had as much to drink as if it had rained, so that streams of it ran past the house.

When Audigier was born, there was great joy throughout the land. There was such a famine that nightingales and other birds no longer sang; instead there was a she-ass that brayed, an old dog that howled, and a one-eyed cat that screeched from hunger.

Poitru, Coquelorde, and Hermengot were the three godmothers; there were no more. They carried the baby to Father Herbout, who was picking off his lice in front of the church and scratching his ass with his right hand. He jumped to his feet when he saw them.

The priest entered in his funeral garb. He put on his finest surplice, which bore a close resemblance to a fishing net. Not a full foot of it was whole. It had come back from the laundry as white as the sweep from a chimney.

The godmothers saw he was taking too long. They didn't need a priest to read the psalter. Nearby there was a ditch under a willow tree where Lady Rainberge used to go to piss. There they plunged the baby three times. They laid him in the skin of a dog that his father had killed a short while ago, so he wouldn't howl any more. Then off went the godmothers without delay.

The infant Audigier was well cared for. He was bathed three times a day in a bucket stinking with piss. They made him a broth of rotten eggs. Then they gave him rotten onions to give him a healthier chest; but he didn't want to eat them unless they were fried in good goat or lamb grease.

He had a large head with small eyes. He was no bigger than a mouse. "Lords," said Rainberge, "behold my son; he will win many battles, for his heart is larger than a mouse."

Now, lords, listen, all of you. I shall tell of a knight named Tirarz, who so loved Rainberge (I'm not joking!) that he took her as his wife. (Believe it; it's true!) The bold and sturdy lady had two sons by him, one named Raier, the other, Avisart. Audigier was the third, the least cowardly, who was the son of Turgibus, that good vassal.

Lords, listen now, without making noise. I shall tell you of Avisart and Raier, who made Audigier, their brother, a knight. They led the boy onto a dungheap, carrying his arms in a basket. They dressed him in a lightweight, white hauberk. It had cost fifteen Venetian pennies a short while before. They laced on his head a steel helmet which had been in hock for three years for ten pence. Tirarz belted on his sword, which was dear to him; he couldn't have wished for a worse servant. He gave him a blow with the palm of his hand on the neck, making him fall to one knee. They brought his fine war-horse up to that place. This was what Audigier really treasured. Audigier mounted it by the stirrup.

When Audigier mounted, there was rejoicing. He struck the horse three blows; at the fourth, he stopped. It had a slender neck, a large head, and a back sharper than the beard of any wheat. "Ah, God!" said Audigier, "What a fine beast! I won't mount it again unless for a celebration or, in mortal warfare, to save my neck; for no one has ever seen such a fine beast."

Audigier sat armed on the war-horse; around him there were more than a thousand people. They began dancing in a ring on the dungheap. There could be seen many carters, many hideous old ladies, many charcoal burners. But there was an old lady of great might; Grinberge was her name, from Valgrifier, ugly, aged, and more hideous than the devil. She was greatly displeased by the joy of the knight, and in order to shame and anger him, the lady uncovered herself without delay and went right into the middle of the dancing to shit.

This greatly grieved Audigier. He swore by God, the Righteous, if he lived until the fields could be mowed, he would go the next day to break down her door; and if he could find the hen house, he would ride off with all the eggs.

The old woman had acted boldly, shitting among the dancing where everyone could see her. Audigier and his relatives threatened her and swore by God the Omnipotent that she would soon pay for it. Quickly they asked who she was. A small boy quietly told them, "Sire, her name is Grinberge (I'm not lying to you!); she's a wicked, old, lying woman. Don't threaten her anymore, for if she shouts for help, there will quickly come more than a hundred old ladies. I think the youngest one is at least a hundred years old, and not one of them has a single tooth. They won't spare your arms."

When Audigier heard this, he waited no longer but quickly turned away from there.

Audigier was armed on Audigon, the best animal belonging to his household. By prime he had ridden a mile and a half. Audigon could go no further that day. Audigier fell off into a bush; until prime he hung there by his spur. When the wind knocked him down onto the sand, the noble man jumped to his feet and drew the sword which hung at his waist. Furiously, he approached the bush and cut off three thorns and a thistle. Thus he proved himself a right noble man.

Audigier rode off in great triumph. No more cowardly man, the story says, ever entered abbey or cloister. He had a pale face, a black head, large shoulders, and an even larger belly. He never had to take an enema, for he had diarrhea in all seasons.

Audigier rode along the pathway. Grinberge had repaired to her house. She knew that she would do battle, for she was provoked because Audigier's relatives had threatened her. She stayed in her house with her household. She had an ill-taught daughter named Bougise who was wrinkled. The girl was ugly and badly shaped.

She had another daughter who was cursed. Her face was the

color of dog-berries. No word of truth ever came out of her mouth, and people said she was a heretic. She had a short, twisted spine.

The third daughter was named Poitron Bernous. Her teeth were small like a wolf's. Often her ass was filthy and covered with shit. Now it so happened, so we read, that Sir Audigier was jealous of it and suffered great pains on its account.

Grinberge was not rich in gold and silver, but she had a little property which she lived off of in noble style, often calling together her neighbors, Houdeart, Gondree, Gertru, and Hersant.

Audigier rode along a road one day when it was already noon. Suddenly Audigier saw Grinberge, yellow and bald. "Old woman," said Audigier, "it's too bad I've seen you." He drew his bare sword out of its scabbard.

"Look now," said Grinberge, "how he sweats!" When Audigier heard this, his blood boiled.

Audigier drew his sword, darker than the juice from an old dung heap when it grows black. He went up to strike Grinberge and gave her a great blow, but he didn't cut either her hair or silk clothing. She seized him by the helmet, bent him toward her, and threw him down in the middle of the road. Then she gleefully leaped on top of him and seated her filthy crack on his face.

Audigier fell armed to the earth. "Let's kill this devil," said Bougise, "who was threatening to chop us up."

"We shall not," said Grinberge, "by Saint Richier. Prisoners should not be killed; but I will make him kiss my ass." Grinberge called out to Count Audigier, "Kiss your neighbor without delay, or you shall not come out of prison for many months."

When he saw he could not avoid it or get out of it, Audigier kissed it with no resistance. Then he remounted his war-horse.

Audigier rode along, greatly distressed. "Alas!" said the good man, "how I am betrayed! I've been badly treated by this filthy old lady. She made me kiss her ass. She has really shamed me if my family and friends find out. But I shall avenge myself here and now. Filthy old traitress, I defy you."

"Audigier," said Grinberge, "to you I say 'bullshit'! You shall have three and a half of my turds for breakfast tomorrow morning and will kiss my ass and asshole as well."

When the vassal heard this, he was greatly troubled. He drew his burnished blade out of its scabbard and rode off toward the hen house. When the old woman saw him, she grew pale. She said to Bougise, "Will he get away?"

"By God," said the girl, "lady, not at all. You go this way, by the house, and I'll go that way, through the garden. If I can catch up with him and hold him, I'll piss right in his face, and he won't need his burnished blade."

When the old woman heard her, she laughed loudly. "By my head," she said, "that's the way to talk."

The old woman, swelled up, turned and ran after Audigier with her mouth hanging open. She caught up with him in a plowed field, and the lady seized him hardily so that his sword fell out of his hand. She threw him off his horse in the middle of the field and swallowed him down like a blessed host. When she felt herself swollen up she crouched down on the ground and opened her asshole wide. Audigier shot out, crying "Onward!"

Then you could have seen Bougise, enraged, coming toward Audigier without delay. She took him by his swollen head and threw him down in the field; and when he had fallen with his mouth open, she hardily pissed on his face. She soaked his body and back. Then she left him in the middle of the field, and the count remounted without delay.

Audigier proudly rode on and came swiftly to his castle. His family gathered around him. His friends and brothers asked, "Where have you been, fair sir, so long? Have you jousted with a knight?"

"No," said Audigier, "I didn't find any. But I found that old woman, damn her! I beat her and bruised her and trampled her. I clambered over her three times on my horse. Then I would have killed her if I hadn't remembered that, in truth, it would have been a sin."

"Sire," said the brothers, "this was a proud deed. You shall conquer lands through your valor, and we shall be honored by you."

The next day in the morning, just before dawn, Audigier rose and proudly mounted Audigon with his shield at his neck, raising his lance. He threatened to kill the old lady and her daughter, Bougise the hunchbacked, because she had treated him so badly. The count rode off, lance lifted, and traveled throughout the morning, looking to his right down in the valley. Then he saw Grinberge where she was washing the guts and odd pieces of a goat. He spurred his war-horse to a gallop, charged suddenly at the old woman, and snatched it out of her hands. When the old lady saw this, she was not happy.

Audigier rode through the field, spurring his horse to go faster, came up to Grinberge, and snatched it out of her hands.* She would be ashamed if she let him do this! She seized him by the helmet, pulled it to her, and led him off to her prison without delay. She imprisoned him under a table.

Alas! Then Audigier was in a strong prison, and Grinberge held him with a neck chain and swore by the Lord God and His holy name that he would never get out of her prison if he did not give her a great ransom. She wanted to have a bushel of beans and a slab of his bacon, and she also wanted a fat hen and for him to kiss first her ass, then her cunt, while she squatted over his face.

"Lady," said Audigier, "we grant it. We shall do all your will. You know well what is suited to such a noble. We shall do your will and your desire; you know very well that I am in your power."

---

* This sort of repetition is a stylistic characteristic of works written in *laisses,* as is "Audigier." It occurs again elsewhere in the tale.

Grinberge uncovered her ass and cunt and squatted down over his face. Shit fell from her ass in great profusion.

While Audigier lay down on a dungheap, Grinberge sat on him, which quite upset him. Twice she made him kiss her ass until it was wiped clean, and it was smeared all over Audigier's lips. "Audigier," said Grinberge, "my ass is wiped."

Grinberge uncovered herself up to the navel and sat down on Audigier—not unwillingly. On his face she seated her ass. When Audigier felt how ill-treated he was, he nearly went out of his mind with rage. "Remove, old whore, your rear."

Grinberge got up and they all laughed, she and her daughters, and six old women. The vassal sorrowfully got on his horse and returned to his own land. Rainberge looked him in the face and said, "Son, you appear pale to me. Where have you been? Tell me, without lying."

"Lady," said Audigier, "let me be. I am slightly ill from fasting too long. Have a dinner prepared."

"Willingly," said the lady, "bold knight. Truly, when I look at you, I don't want to hide from you that in your face and features you look very much like your father Turgibus, who was so valiant."

The meal was soon ready. There were three old, salted vultures, which the cook had prepared for him, and old, rotten onions. With this Audigier was reinvigorated.

Audigier had a cook whose name was Hertauz. Before, his skin was peeling; behind, he was bald. Scurvy dripped from him down to his toes; and when he had put his eggs in his morter and scratched his head, the flour fell in the morter, helping him make his eggs. Audigier ate his fine morsels—vultures, plums, and crows—until his great sorrow had passed away. Then he was healed—the noble vassal—of the great pains he had had and the sufferings; he was cared for because of his painful combat.

Lady Rainberge was overjoyed that Audigier had begun his

chivalry. "Fair son," said Rainberge, "do you want a girl, a god-daughter whom I have raised? She is Troncecrevace, sister of Maltrecie. She has nails longer than a magpie's beak. Never once in her life has she washed her hands or once wiped the crease of her ass. I never remember it when she shits."

"Ah, God!" said Audigier. "What a companion! I wish to make her my beloved."

"Lady," said Audigier, "show her to me. I am so shaken by love for her that I shall go out of my mind if I don't see her."

"My faith," said Rainberge, "willingly. This very night I shall have her dine with you. The three of us will have two sets of goat guts. Remember to drink you know what, for you won't drink if I can't."

"Lady," said Audigier, "I believe you. Your ass has always held good faith with me. Do not complain when I drink the shit. Now lead my beloved before me."

"Audigier," said Rainberge, "here is your wife. Yesterday she ate turnips and onion stew and drank a great bowl of broth. If you had drunk in the fumes, you would never have cared again about a blow with a sword."

"Lady," said Audigier, "this pleases me. Human flesh is worthless unless bewitched."

Audigier took the girl by the mantle and led her out into a field. He had her squat down in the loveliest part of it and put the ring on her finger while shitting. She shit for him such a heap that it filled his hat more than three times. "Lady," said Audigier, "this delights me, that we should well fertilize our field. The fumes are rising up to my head and the fragrance is wafted to my nostrils."

Audigier did not wish to hold his wedding in a meadow or in a wood or on the banks of a stream or in a leafy forest. Instead he held it in an old, plowed-up field where sows and hogs had been. They spread out the cloths from a bag full of holes which a noble butcher had loaned them, in which he had wrapped up his fat.

Then they ate their rats with lard and had good chives mixed with chicken shit.

"Ah, God," said Audigier, "how we've dined! This meat and drink is savory indeed; never was a count so well satisfied."

The wedding of Audigier was a grand affair with many princes and gentle folk. Instead of fine herbs and spices, the floors were sprinkled with men's turds. There were as many as a hundred *jongleurs*. The next day they came to be paid and Audigier gleefully gave each of them thirty goat droppings. Then the court broke up, and the people went off.

Notes to "Audigier"

The unspeakable "Audigier"! First published a century and a half ago, it was only republished, with profuse apologies, by Omer Jodogne in 1960. When not ignored by scholars, it has aroused them to outraged denunciations. The medieval public evidently felt otherwise. Audigier was a well-known figure in the literature of the period; and though his name occurs in distinctively lower-class literature such as the *sotes chansons* (it turns up as an example of bad taste in Adam de la Halle's *Robin et Marion*), it also appears in writings belonging to the noble milieu. He is mentioned in the epics of *Octavian, Doon de Nanteuil, Aiol*, and in the *Roman de la Violette* by Gerbert de Montreil. The nobility, it would seem, were amused.

Written at the end of the twelfth century, when epics were still being composed, the tale of Audigier is told in assonating laisses rather than the rhymed couplets of romance; yet the story itself obviously draws heavily on romance. It is an outrageous scatological parody of the adventures of a knightly father and son (the sagas of Cligés and of Arthur himself, to name only two, included their fathers' adventures).

In "Audigier" we have a hint of the influences working on Rabelais much later and a vision of what might have resulted had that writer chosen to concentrate exclusively on the excremental current running through his work. The land of *Cocuce* is an open sewer. The scenery is littered with dungheaps, and excrement is the coin of the realm. The tale of Audigier is a veritable *chanson de merde.*

In fact, the author's concentration on excrement suggests that perhaps the subject had a deeper interest for him than we might at first suspect. To be sure, the work is a burlesque, a grotesque satire of knightly adventures; but it may also be a piece of coprophiliac pornography.

At any rate, after *Audigier,* let no one speak of the impeccably pure tastes of the medieval nobility and claim that vulgarity or obscenity is inevitably the mark of the bourgeoisie.

Auberée, The Old Bawd

JEHAN RENART (?)

Whoever wishes to gather round will hear me tell a fine tale which I have taken a lot of trouble with. I put it into rhyme, line by line, just as it happened in the town of Compiègne. There was a wise, courteous, and wealthy citizen who lived in the town. He was anxious to honor the poor as well as the rich and was never miserly or greedy in all his youth. His valor and his generosity were spoken of as far away as Beauvoisin.

He had a poor neighbor who had a pretty daughter. The young man got to know her and courted her for a long while. She told him flatly that he was wasting his effort if he didn't want to marry her; but if he wished to have her as his wife, properly, she would be very happy. "Gladly," said the young man, "that's what I want. I'm delighted."

He gave her his promise and said no more. He went back to his house and spoke to his father, telling him how things were. But his father argued with him, reproached and reproved him: "Fine son," he said, "speak no more of this. She has nothing to do with you. She isn't worthy to remove your shoes. I'll see you advance in life, whatever it costs me. I want you to associate with the finest people in the land. I'm shocked at your folly, wanting to marry

SOURCE: T. B. W. Reid, ed., *Twelve Fabliaux* (Manchester, Eng.: Manchester University Press, 1958), pp. 54–69.

He had a son, a young man, who squandered many a denier throughout his adolescence.

such a girl. You'll deserve to be killed if you ever speak of it again!"

The young man saw by these words that his father disregarded him and would grant him nothing. Love, who rules his subjects, had seized and inflamed the young man, so that he thought of nothing but the maiden.

Three days later it happened that the wife of a rich citizen died; but before the lady had been dead a month the citizen, quickly consoling himself on the advice of his friends, began speaking to the father about the lovely, gentle maiden who was beloved by the one I mentioned before. This citizen I'm speaking of succeeded so well that he got the maiden in his power and married her the next day.

This did not please the young man at all, who thought of her day and night. Everything he saw pained him. He hated the solace offered by people; he hated his silver, his gold, and his great riches. He swore that he had been contemptible to believe his father. He had to suffer for his great wealth. He thought this way for a long time, not knowing how to think any other way which might bring him some comfort.

He had a costume made of wool and dyed in scarlet, checked with green. Each part was made with long tails. The surcoat was edged with fine squirrel fur. He himself had used to be handsome and noble looking, but now he had a pale, wan face. One day he went out of his house with his head wrapped in a mantle, enjoying walking along by the castles, until he came to the house of his love. It was the season when it is as hot as it is in August. He thought to himself that he must devise, whatever it cost, some way to speak to his love. He carefully watched and waited.

Then he saw the house of an old seamstress. He crossed the street to where she was seated at the window. She, who was full of deceit, asked him how he was and what had happened to him, for he used to be cheerful and most highly praised. The old woman's name was Auberée. There was no lady so well locked up that she couldn't pull her by her cord. The young man sat down by her and told her word for word how he loved the woman who was her neighbor. If she could arrange for him to gain possession of her, she would have fifty pounds.

She, who would not fail, said to him, "I don't think she is so well guarded that I can't have her speak to you occasionally from the door to the ground. Hurry and go find me the money and I'll think about this business."

He ran and opened a cupboard where there was a good deal of money which his father had saved. He took the money and returned quickly to Auberée. He showed her the fifty pounds, but he wasn't through yet. He would have to add another contribution.

"Now give me your surcoat," said the old woman. "Hurry!" Not wanting to contradict her, he did what the old woman told him to, so much did love rule him. She folded the surcoat tightly and put it under her arm, then got up from her seat, put on a short mantle, and ran to the house. It was a market day, and the old woman had carefully noted that the husband was not in.

"May God be in your house," she said. "God be with you, sweet lady! And may God have mercy on the other lady who died, and who troubles my heart. She honored me for many years."

"Welcome, Lady Auberée," said the lady; "come sit down."

"My lady, I've come to see you because I want to get to know you. I haven't crossed this threshold since the other lady died. She never refused me anything I asked her for. In fact, even if I asked her to do something really troublesome, she immediately did it, by my head. She was so good."

"Lady Auberée, do you need anything? If you do, tell us."

"Lady," she said, "I've come to you because my daughter has a pain in her side and wants some of your white wine and just one of your good loaves, the smallest one you have. My God! I'm so ashamed, but the girl pleaded with me so much that I had to ask you. I've never been a beggar before, but I can't help myself now, by my soul."

"You shall have whatever there is here in this house," said the lady.

Then she, who was clever, sat down beside the woman. "I'm certainly glad to hear you speak this way. How is your lord? Is he pleasant toward you? Ah! How he loved the other one! He gave her great delight. I would like to see your bed; then I would know for sure if you are bedded as richly as the first lady was."

The lady rose up, and with Auberée following her they both entered a nearby bedroom. It was filled with many things. There were gray and silver furs and cloth of silk and samite. She showed her a large bed and told the old woman, "Here my lord lies, and I lie beside him."

The bed was made of white straw covered with a quilt. The old woman had a sharp needle with a thimble in the surcoat which she had under her arm, held tightly close to her side. When the lady of the house had shown her all her belongings, the old woman hastily shoved the surcoat under the quilt.

"Certainly," said she, "I haven't seen such a fine bed since Pentecost. It seems to me he must be happier with you than he was with the other one."

Then they went out of the bedroom with the old woman still talking away. The lady gave her a pot full of wine, a loaf, a slice from a side of bacon, and a large pot of peas. The lady was completely fooled by Auberée, for she didn't know her; nor did she know her guile and deceit.

Now I must speak of the citizen who returned alone from the town, having done his business. He wanted to sleep for a little while. In one place under the quilt he felt the bulge of the surcoat. He began to feel it with his hand, not knowing what it was that was bothering him. Then he raised the quilt and drew out the surcoat. He was so terribly shocked that if someone had stuck a

knife in his body, right in the side, he wouldn't have drawn a drop
of blood. "Alas!" he said. "I've been betrayed by her who never
loved me!"

Then he ran to the door and shut it. He took up the surcoat,
overcome by jealousy (which is worse than a toothache), and
looked at it inside and out, until it almost seemed as if he wanted
to buy it. But he was aching in every limb, full of anger and wrath.
"Alas!" he said. "What can this surcoat mean?" And he said that,
by his soul, it belonged to his wife's lover. She had consented to
give him solace and had felt his flanks. He took it and stored it
away then leaned on the bed and thought what he could do. But
the more he thought about this affair, the more his suffering
increased.

He was thus until night, when he saw the gates close down the
street. Then he took his wife and drove her out through the door
from the house. She, who didn't know of what she was accused,
was almost overwhelmed with grief.

Along came Lady Auberée, the old woman, who looked at her
and said, "My lovely girl, God save you! What are you doing
here?"

"Ah! Lady Auberée, help me. My husband is angry with me, but
I don't know why. I don't know what anybody has told him. Do
me the favor of going with me to my father's."

"What?" she said. "By the Holy Father, I wouldn't do that for
anything. Do you want your father to accuse you? He will believe
you've done your husband some wrong, committed some villainy
with your body for which he threw you out, or that he caught you
in the act with your lover. But the villain is drunk, I hope. He'll be
over it tomorrow. In good faith, I advise you to come with me.
The streets are empty of people. I employed the bread, wine,
meat, and peas better than you think. I would like to return in full
the help and service. Everything will be done as you wish, whatever you want. All you have to do is ask. You'll be completely

hidden in an out-of-the-way room, and not a soul will know you are there, until your lord will have gotten completely over his drunkenness."

Then they made their way, with the old woman leading her to her house. "My dear," she said, "You could be here safely for a week, and nobody would know about it."

Then they sat down to eat, but the lady refused and said, please God, she would not eat until she knew why this shame had been brought upon her. At these words Lady Auberée left off preaching to her and led her into a nearby bedroom to sleep in white sheets and a fine quilt. The old woman covered her well. She did not leave the room open, but locked the door securely with the key.

Then she quietly slipped out of her house and hurried to the young man, who was not sleeping, but turning over and over in his bed. He greatly feared the old woman would forget the promise she had made him. He sighed deeply from his heart and sat up naked in his bed. Then he got up and went to lean on a windowsill. The old woman, who wanted to earn her pay and serve the young man well, turned neither to left nor right. She found the young man at the window, and he asked her what news she had.

"I have good news, fine news; for I've caught your love in my nets, and you can have solace with her until after this time tomorrow."

The young man, whom the old lady had served well, did not delay. They quietly went down the steps and set off together. The lady had barely fallen asleep when he who desired her took off his shoes and undressed. "Lady," he asked, "what if she resists and cries out? What shall I say? I want to do what you advise."

"I shall advise you rightly," said the old woman. "Go, lie down, and if she is reluctant, let her shout. All the more, lift the sheets and climb in. As soon as she feels you, things will go otherwise. Then you'll see her grow quiet, and you can do your pleasure."

The young man went to the bed and slipped in beside the woman and gently drew near her. Then she, who was very weary, awoke. When she felt him, she jumped out of bed; but he embraced her and said, "My dear, come closer, for I am your sweet love whom you cast into pain. But I have succeeded, thank God, in getting you all alone with me in this locked room. I have greatly desired you."

"My faith," she said, "this won't do you any good. I'll shout so loud that soon everybody from this street will come running here."

"But certainly that's useless," he said; "for it would only mean shame for you if everyone—noble and common—were to see you and me nude, side by side. Now it is almost midnight and not one of them wouldn't believe that I hadn't taken my will of your body. It would be much better to conceal this from those outside our meeting so that no one but the three of us will know it."

Then he drew her to him again and put his arms around her white and slender sides, kissing her mouth and face. The lady didn't know what to do. It would be better for her to keep quiet than to receive such a reputation and ill-fame among her neighbors; and it would cause her nothing but shame. The young man assuaged her fears and quieted her, embracing and kissing her. Then the two of them together did that for which they had been brought together.

In the morning, at the crack of dawn, Auberée got up and prepared as best she could roast pork and capons. Then they sat down to eat. None of them refused; they ate and drank a great deal. Both of them were happy to accept Lady Auberée's services.

When it was time to be shut up again and turn to solace, Lady Auberée prepared things for them in the way she knew pleased them, which wasn't exactly what pleased her. That night they had great solace, lying in each others' arms. They stayed awake all night until matins were rung at the abbey of Saint Corneille.

As soon as she had heard the bell, Lady Auberée woke up, got dressed and prepared herself, and went to the bed where they lay, talking of their love together. "Get up, my dear," she said, "and you and I shall go to the chapel of Saint Corneille. It's necessary now to be reconciled with your husband."

This displeased the young man, but he didn't dare contradict her. The old woman said to him, "Let me do what I want. You will regain your beloved and your delight again."

Auberée had eight candles, each of which was more than six feet long. She and the lady went out of her house with them and came before the altar and the statue of Our Lady. Auberée, who was very wise, had the lady lie down on the ground and forbid her to care about her dispute more than three nuts' worth. The old woman had made four crosses. She lit the candles from a burning lamp, one by one. She put one of the crosses at her head, one at her feet, one at her right, and the fourth at her left. Then she went off, assuring her, "Don't be afraid of anything. Be careful, whatever happens, and don't move until I come back. Meanwhile, just lie there."

"Lady," she said, "gladly."

Then the old woman turned away and made straight for the house of the citizen, who was grieving because of his wife and didn't know what to do. She arrived and knocked and kicked to wake him up; and he, who was listening and was eager to hear something that might cheer him up, ordered the door to be opened. He asked Lady Auberée to enter. She said, "Where is that wretch, that scoundrel, that boor?"

"Lady Auberée, welcome," he said. "What do you wish at this hour?"

She quickly replied, "Alas, I'll tell you my dream. This night I dreamed a terrible dream which woke me up from fright. I got dressed and went to the abbey church; I was so upset. And there, in front of the altar of Our Lady, I saw your wife stretched out. I was amazed, for I didn't know what this could mean. At her head, at her feet, at her right and left, I saw candles burning. There I saw your wife lying before the altar in prayer. You've committed a great crime against her, and you'll beat your breast about it yet. Should she be all alone there like that, such a beautiful woman?

"Cross yourself, Auberée! I'm in despair about this. I think it's a great marvel that she's keeping watch this way. Here is this tender child who was born only yesterday, and who ought in the morning to be sleeping here under the bed curtains, and you send her to matins! To matins! Alas, you sinner! May the hand of God the Spirit cross and bless and rebless me. Do you want to make her one of those women who are always running to church? May the damned fire burn whoever sends a young woman off this way!" Thus the old woman led him away from his evil thoughts.

If it hadn't been for the surcoat, he would have thought nothing but good of her; but he was still suspicious. The citizen said, "Are you telling the truth?"

"Get up, and you can see," said the old woman, "if I'm lying to you." He quickly arose, not caring to lie there anymore; and the two of them went to the church. There he found his wife, just as Auberée had said. The citizen drew near her, raised her by the hand, and told her he had wronged her through drunkenness.

Both of them returned home and went back to bed. The lady covered her head, for she wished to sleep. She little cared about her husband's anger so long as he didn't know anything; and the husband for his part thought his wife had an empty head to weep and watch so, continually praying night and day before the altar for her lord. Thus the citizen lay beside his wife until day appeared and the sun rose high. Then the citizen dressed and put on his shoes and left his wife lying. He went out of his house and crossed his head and body.

Lady Auberée jumped out and shouted in a loud voice, "Thirty sous! By the True Cross! Now I don't care if I live any longer! Thirty sous! Miserable wretch! Thirty sous! Alas, what shall I do?

Thirty sous! Where will I get them? God, I'm miserable! Thirty sous! Alas, woe! This is a disaster!"

Along came the citizen and saw Lady Auberée shouting up and down, "Thirty sous! Alas, thirty sous! The provost will come and take what little I have. That's the dream I dreamed."

"Tell me, may God aid you," said the amazed citizen, "why you are so unhappy. By my head, I want to know."

She said, "I'll tell you, and not a word of it will be a lie. A young man came here the day before yesterday and gave me his surcoat to be mended and repaired. A splinter had ripped three or four squirrel skins from it. I took it and went along sewing on it at my leisure, for I felt a little tired. Thus I unhappily took my sewing with me that day, out of my house. My property is in danger since I've lost the surcoat. I am so upset I don't know where I am. What can I do except run away? I don't know any other course. If they try to treat me this way, I'll excommunicate them Sunday in all the churches. I really didn't need to suffer such a loss. Good sir, listen to something else. If God lets me live until Christmas, I left my thimble hanging with my needle in that surcoat. I would be indebted to anybody who gave it back to me. The young man keeps coming every day, bothering me and demanding me to give him either thirty sous or the surcoat; but I simply cannot give it back to him."

"Tell me, Lady Auberée, were you in my house a while ago?"

"Yes, sire, to gain a little relief for my daughter, who had a headache. It was the day before yesterday; now I remember. I found the lady in her bedroom, combing her hair. I saw a quilt spread out over the bed. My eyes had never seen such a pretty one before. I dawdled there so long that I fell asleep on the quilt. The lady woke me up and willingly prepared the things I had asked her for. Then I went off. That's how that day went; but I don't know, alas, what became of the surcoat, except that I suspect that I may have forgotten it on the bed."

When the citizen heard this news, he was delighted. If he found the thimble he would be happier than he had ever been in his life. He was anxious to see the proof. He went to his house, opened a closet, and drew out the surcoat which he had stored away. When he found the thimble and needle attached to it, he couldn't have been made happier if he had been given all of Apulia.

"By the Lord God," he said, "now I know for sure that the old woman wasn't lying, for I've found her sewing." The citizen was happy about what had happened and rejoiced. He took the surcoat back to Auberée and rid himself of it. Thus the old woman delivered the citizen from his evil thoughts; for he thought no more of it once he had gotten rid of the surcoat. She had the fifty pounds, and she deserved her pay. All three of them were served as they wished.

By this fabliau I wish to show that few women misbehave with their bodies unless because of another woman. That is the correct path, if someone wishes to seduce a woman who is clean, pure, and chaste. And thus our fabliau ends.

Notes to "Auberée, the Old Bawd"

In the early thirteenth century someone, perhaps Jehan Renart, adapted a tale into French which had a long and distinguished history. The old bawd with her coat had wandered through the medieval Near East in various collections including the famous *Book of the Seven Wise Masters*, through the Latin *Disciplina Clericalis* of Petrus Alphonsus (itself translated into French), to our present author. Her story belonged to the body of Oriental tales which was predominately the property of the nobility.

The bawd is a figure foreign to the native French fabliau. The vulgar affairs of priests and *vilains* seldom required a go-between, and her services were mainly useful to young men of a social class somewhat removed from the world of the bourgeois fabliau proper. Yet the bawd as a literary figure is of the utmost importance. Retaining her own identity, she reaches her greatest triumph in *La Celestina* by the early sixteenth-century Spanish author Fernando de Rojas; but she also influenced the figure of La Vielle ("The Old Woman") of *The Romance of the Rose* and is reflected in aspects of Chaucer's Wife of Bath.

Auberée is not a fully developed character as these are, but she possesses the cunning and hypocrisy and the garrulousness characteristic of bawds in the literature of several centuries. (The tradition may be traced back as far as the *Kama Sutra* and to whatever period it is assigned.) Her intricate plot works as successfully as a Rube Goldberg device for bringing lovers together and soothing the jealous husband.

The milieu is bourgeois, the "moral" is not of the noblest, and the author clearly labels his work a fabliau. Yet the story emerged from aristocratic circles and probably remained popular there. It appears in no less than six manuscripts which were probably compiled at the order of noblemen.

"Auberée" forms a transition between the predominantly courtly works which we have been treating and the sort of tale usually regarded as distinctively bourgeois. We have seen the lay and romance lapse into farce and fabliau; the "bourgeois" genres often reflect the tastes of the noble audiences which, in fact, enjoyed them. It seems clear that it is impossible to label these tales as belonging to precise social classes.

- the figure of the bawd
- women misbehave w/ their bodies due to another women
- "go-between" : Lunette

Boivin of Provins

HIMSELF*

Boivin was a fine glutton. He thought he would go to the fair at Provins and get himself talked about. He did as he had planned, clad in a drugget gown, with cape, coat, and surcoat, all in one, I believe; and he put a coarse cloth cap on his head. His shoes were not the laced kind but of strong, tough cowhide. He, who knew many tricks, let his beard grow without shaving it for a month or more. He took a toolbag in his hand so he would seem more like a peasant. He bought a large purse and put twelve deniers in it, for he had no more.

He went straight to the street of the whores, right in front of the house of Mabile, who knew more tricks and ruses than any woman alive. He sat down on a stump in front of the house, laid his toolbag by him, and turned his back to the door. Now you shall hear what he did next.

"My faith," he said, "I know what I ought to do. Since I'm away from the fair in a good place, far from people, I ought to count my money all by myself. That's what wise men do. I got thirty-nine sous from Rouget, and Girault, who helped me sell my

SOURCE: Jean Rychner, *Contribution à l'étude des fabliaux: Variantes, remaniements, dégradations,* 2 vols. (Neuschatel: Faculté des lettres and Genève: Droz, 1960), II: viii, A.

* Thus the manuscript. A statement at the conclusion of the tale indicates it was rather written by the *prévôt* of Provins. See page 88.

two oxen, got twelve deniers of it. May he go hang for keeping my deniers! That rascal kept twelve of them. I did pretty well by him. But, that's the way it is; no use complaining about it. He'll come looking for my oxen when he wants to plow his land and sow his barley. Damn my throat if he ever gets anything out of me! I know how to put him in his place. Shame on him and all his heirs!

"But I'll get back to my own affairs. I got nineteen sous from Sorin. I wasn't crazy to get that; for my friend Sir Gautier wouldn't have given me so many deniers. That's why I was smart to sell at the fair. He wanted credit, and I've got my goods. Nineteen and thirty-nine sous, that's how much my oxen were sold for. By God! I don't know how much that adds up to! If I had to count it all together, I couldn't tell the sum. If I had to count it, I wouldn't know the half of it unless I used peas or beans, a pea for each sou; then I'd know the whole amount. But Sirout told me that I got fifty sous for my oxen. He counted them out, and I got them; but I don't know if he tricked me or stole some from me.

"Then he gave me as much again for two bushels of wheat and my mare and my pigs, plus the wool from my lambs. Two times fifty are one hundred, that's what the boy who counted it said. He said it amounted to five pounds. Now I won't let my full purse be emptied in my lap."

The pimps in the house said, "Come here, Mabile, listen. Those deniers will certainly be ours if you bring that peasant in here. They're of hardly any use to him."

Mabile said, "Leave him in peace. Let him count it all out, piece by piece, so that none of it will escape me. I'll give you every denier, I swear, or you can tear my eyes out, if he has one left to count."

But I believe the game will go otherwise than she thought; for the peasant was counting and going over just the twelve deniers that he had. He counted them back and forth and said, "Now that's twenty sous five times. I had better keep them; that's smart.

But I keep thinking about one thing. If I had my sweet niece, who was my sister Tiece's daughter, she would be mistress of my wealth. She foolishly went out of the country to another land. I've looked for her many days in many lands, in many towns. Ah, my sweet niece, Mabile! You were so well born! Then where did you get such an idea? All three of my children are dead, along with my wife, Siersant. I'll never be happy again until the hour that I see my sweet niece. Then I'll become a white monk,* and she will be mistress of my wealth. She can have a rich husband."

Thus he complained and wept. Mabile jumped up, sat down by him, and said, "Good man, where do you come from, and what is your name?"

"My name is Fouchier de la Brouce. But you resemble my sweet niece more than any woman alive!"

She fainted onto the stump. When she got up again, she said, "Now I have what I've longed for." Then she embraced him and kissed him on the face and mouth. She couldn't seem to get enough.

And he, who knew how to deceive, clenched his teeth and sighed, "Lovely niece, I cannot tell you the great joy I have in my heart. Are you my sister's daughter?"

"Yes, sire, of Lady Tiece."

"I have been without you for a long time," said the peasant, "without comfort." He embraced her tightly and kissed her. Thus the two of them were joyful.

In the middle of this, two pimps came out of the house. The pimps asked, "Is this good man from your town?"

"Yes, it's my uncle," said Mabile, "that I've told you so much about." She turned slightly toward them with her tongue in her cheek, making a face at the pimps.

"Is this your uncle, then?"

"Yes, it is."

* A Cistercian.

"You can be proud of him and he of you, without a doubt. As for you," said the pimps, "good man, we are completely at your service. By Saint Peter, the good apostle, you shall have the lodgings of Saint Julian. There's not a man from here to Gien who has finer ones." They took Sir Fouchier by the arms and led him into their house.

"Quickly," said Mabile, "friends, go buy geese and capons."

"Lady," they said, "give us something. We don't have a bit of money."

"Quiet!" she said. "Villains! Put up your mantles and your coats as security. This peasant will redeem your pledges. Your pledges will be safe, for you will get more than a hundred sous."

What more can I say? The two pimps, however they procured them, quickly brought two fat capons and two geese. Boivin made a face at them as soon as they turned away.

Mabile told them, "Be good, and get them ready." Then you could see the pimps plucking the capons and geese. Ysane made the fire and did all the other things she had to do.

Mabile couldn't keep quiet and had to speak to her peasant: "Good uncle, are your wife and my two nephews well? They must be fine young men by now."

The peasant answered, "Dear niece, all three of them are dead. I almost died of grief myself. Now you will be my only comfort in my country, in our town."

"Alas!" said Mabile. "I'll go out of my mind. Alas! If it had been after dinner, it wouldn't have been so bad. Alas! This very night I saw this happen as I slept."

"Lady, the capons are done and the geese roasted," said Ysane, hurrying along. "My sweet lady, go wash; leave off your weeping."

They poked the peasant, and he, who wasn't blind, saw that they were mocking him. The pimps said, "Good sir, you are not wise; that's my opinion. Let the dead rest, cling to the living."

Then they sat down to the table where there was truly an abundance of food. There were plenty of good wines, and they made the peasant drink enough to make him drunk and to deceive him. But he feared nothing. He put his hand under his cape and pretended to reach for his money.

Mabile said, "What are you after, dear uncle? Tell me."

"Good niece, I know, I can see that this dinner cost a great deal. I'll pay twelve deniers." But Mabile and the pimps swore that he wouldn't spend a single denier.

They took away the table when they had eaten, and Mabile gave the two pimps leave to go out. "If you liked the birds you had for dinner, brace yourself for supper." The two pimps went away, closing the door after them.

Mabile began asking questions: "My dear uncle, don't conceal from me whether you've been keeping company with any other woman since your wife died. To suffer too much for a woman is stupid. It's a madness, just as much as going hungry."

"Niece, it's been seven whole years."

"Has it really been that long?"

"At least! I just haven't felt like it."

"Quiet, uncle. God bless you! Look at me." And she beat her breast three times. "Uncle, I've sinned terribly. I deceived my parents. I would have gotten a lot of money if I had sold my maidenhead. But you will have it; I want you to." She winked at Ysane, to cut his purse. But the peasant thought of cutting it first, before Ysane. Sir Fouchier took the purse and cut it off, and his wallet as well. He put them in his breast, next to the bare skin, then turned around.

He turned to Ysane, and they approached each other, then went to lay down on the mattress. Ysane lay down first and begged Sir Fouchier not to hurt her. Then he had to raise her ass-covering to do the job. He removed her chemise; he began to stiffen his lance, and she to search for the purse. While she was looking, he embraced her and stabbed her with the point of his prick. He put it in her cunt up to the balls, and banged her ass, and rolled it until he had finished fucking. He raised his pants and saw the two purse-straps hanging down.

"Alas!" he said. "I'm a poor wretch! It's a bad day for me. Niece, my purse has been cut; that woman took it from me."

Mabile heard this and was glad, for she thought it was true and coveted the money. She opened the door. "Peasant," she said, "get out!"

"But get my purse back for me."

"I'll get you a rope to hang yourself. Get out of my house right now, or I'll get a stick!" And she took up a live coal in her two hands.

Then the peasant went out, not caring to be beaten, and the door was shut behind him. People gathered around, and he showed them all that his purse had been cut.

Mabile asked for it from Ysane. "Hand it over, quick, before the peasant goes to the provost."

"By the faith I owe Saint Nicholas," said Ysane, "I don't have it. I searched and looked for it all over."

"Filthy whore, look out, or I'll break all your teeth! Didn't I see the two purse-straps hanging that you cut? You think you can have it for yourself? If you say one more word to me . . . filthy whore, give it here, now!"

"Lady, how can I give you," asked Ysane, "what I don't have?"

Mabile dragged her by the hair, which wasn't short, and knocked her to the ground. She hit her with fists and feet, making her fart and shit.

"By God, whore, this isn't necessary."

"Lady, leave me alone! I'll go look for them until, if I can, I find them. Let me go do that."

"Go," she said, "and hurry!"

Mabile shook the mattress, hoping to find the purse. "Lady,

listen to me!" said Ysane. "May I lose my body and soul if I ever saw the purse. You can kill me if I did."

"By God, whore, you will die." She pulled her to her feet by her hair and clothes, and she cried out, "Help! Help!"

When her pimps heard this, they quickly ran there. In a rush they kicked in the door with their feet, making the hinges fly. They seized Mabile by the hair and even tore it out. Her clothes were so torn that her ass was bare. They took her by the hair and gave her hard blows with their fists in the face and on the cheeks, until they were black and blue.

But she had help, for her friends, having heard her shout, entered in the fray. They immediately took on two gluttons. Then you could see the house fill up with pimps and whores, and everyone getting into it. You could see hair torn, coals flying, clothes ripped, and people falling on top of each other. The merchants ran to see those who had reddened heads. It was a great combat. People who were hardly gentle got involved. They came in with gray robes and got red heads and clothes to mend.

Boivin went straight to the provost and told him the truth, word for word. The provost listened closely, for he was a great lover of lechery. He had him tell his tale often to his relatives and friends, who all enjoyed it and laughed. Boivin stayed three whole days. The provost, who made this fable at Provins, then gave Boivin ten sous of his own money. That is the end of the tale of Boivin.

Notes to "Boivin of Provins"

Boivin de Provins is very closely related to the farce. Composed largely of dialogue, it could be easily converted into a play and may well have been presented in a semidramatic way by *jongleurs*. The protagonist is a *vilain*, the lowest sort of commoner, and the author's attitude toward him may well reflect bourgeois snobbery.

Those attitudes could also reflect noble snobbery, of course. Besides the tale as here translated, there exists another version in which some of the passages tending to degrade the characters have been moderated, much of the obscenity is removed, and there is less violence. Jean Rychner suggests (I: 81–83) that this latter version may have been written by a bourgeois anxious to avoid offending his audience.

The author of the "bourgeois" version also deletes this author's parody of courtly literature, perhaps because it would be meaningless to an audience uninterested in *belles lettres*, looking only for a good belly laugh. The battle of whores and pimps is carefully modeled on epic combats of the most respectable sort, including all the proper terms.

The claim of the author that his story is autobiographical is open to serious doubt, but certainly possible. The tale is not obviously derived from any standard literary motifs, apart from the epic allusions. Perhaps the provost mentioned at the end of the tale was actually the author.

Aloul

Whoever wants to hear the tale of Aloul, as the story is told, can hear plenty of it, unless he can't hear straight. Aloul was a rich peasant, but he was very miserly and stingy. He never wished for the really good things in life, but loved coins above everything, setting his whole mind on them. He had a lovely, gentle wife, whom he had recently married. A subvassal had given her to him because of the wealth surrounding him. Aloul loved her deeply.

The story says that Aloul was jealous and guarded his wife closely. Now jealousy is an evil thing. Aloul had an unhappy life, for he could never be quite sure. This proves he was a fool, acting in such a way. Aloul had plenty to do if he wanted to watch over her all of the time. Let me tell you what it was like. If the lady went to the church, she had no other escort than Aloul, no matter what happened. If she saw anyone other than Aloul, he was immediately suspected of immoral conversation.

This greatly displeased the lady, and when she saw how it was she said to herself that it would be too bad if she didn't deceive him the first time she had time and a place. She could not sleep by day or night, and she hated Aloul and his pleasure. She didn't

SOURCE: Anatole de Montaiglon and Gaston Raynaud, eds., *Recueil général et complet des fabliaux des XIIIe et XIVe siècles*, 6 vols. (Paris: Librarie des bibliophiles, 1872–1890), I: xxiv.

know what to do nor how take her revenge on Aloul, who so wrongfully mistrusted her. The lady rested or slept but little.

She had been in this exile a long time, when finally it was the sweet month of April, when the weather is mild and gentle for all people and for lovers. The nightingale sings so brightly in the branches at dawn that everyone's heart is moved to love.

The lady, having watched long, rose up and went out into the orchard. In her bare feet she went through the dew, wrapped in a fur-lined cloak with a large mantle over it. That morning the priest had risen at the same hour. He was their next door neighbor, and there was only a little wood between them. It was a lovely morning; the weather was mild and gentle. The priest entered and saw the lady with her well-shaped body. You may be sure that it pleased him, for he would willingly have laid her. In fact, he would have bet his robe that he would have his will with her. Wisely, he went forward, quite unabashed.

"Lady," he said, "good day to you. Why have you risen this morning?"

"Sire," she said, "the dew is good and healthful in this weather. It is very soothing, so physicians say."

"Lady," he said, "I can well believe it, for it is good to get up at dawn. But one should breakfast on a vegetable which I know of. Look at it in here, where I can't see it. It is short, with a large root, but it is very fine medicine. There is no better for a woman's body."

"Sire, open your legs," said the lady, "if it please you, and show me if it is there."

"Lady," he said, "here you may find it." Then he opened his legs and stood in front of the lady. "Lady," he said, "sit down now, for we must gather it."

And the lady granted him everything, not understanding his allegory. (My God! If Aloul, who is lying in his bed, knew of this adventure!) The lady quickly sat down and the priest lowered his pants (for he was expert at doing this). He took the lady and laid her back and taught her all about the medicine, and she slipped out from under him.

"Sire," she said, "get up! Flee from here. My God! What shall I do? I shall never believe a priest again."

The priest jumped to his feet, greatly eased. "Lady," he said, "there is no more to do. I am your beloved and your lover. From now on I wish to do all your will."

"Sire," she said, "be careful to conceal this affair well, and I shall give you so much of my wealth that you will always be rich. By my faith, for two whole years Aloul has put me in such distress that I have never had joy or happiness. He is so jealous of me that I hate his very life, for he has shamed me many times. Whoever watches and spies on his wife is a fool. From now on Aloul can say, if he wants to speak the truth, that he is a cuckold. From now on I wish to be your mistress. When the moon has set, come without delay, and I will be ready to receive you and give you ease."

"Lady, my deepest thanks," said the priest. "Let us part for now so that Sir Aloul won't surprise us. Think of me; I shall think of you."

With that, they parted. Each went off without delay; she to her husband, who was very troubled.

"Lady," he asked, "where have you been?"

"Sire," she replied, "down there, in the orchard."

"What?" he said, "without my permission? You don't fear me much; that's what I think."

And the lady kept silent, for she did not care to reply. But Aloul cursed and swore that if she did it again he would cause her shame and pain. Then he got up, pensive and angry. He was much afraid some whoring was going on. (Jealousy leads him on, making him do all her will.)

He went here and there through his manor, trying to see if his wife had hidden anyone anywhere, until he entered a garden. The weather was mild and the morning bright. He looked and saw that the dew was somewhat trampled on here and there in the orchard. Then he grew angry in his heart. He went forward until he came to a place where his foot slipped, where his wife had been made love to, and this caused his foot to slip.

He looked all around and saw the place where heels had struck, and toes. Now Aloul was terribly upset, for he knew everything for certain. The place made it manifest that his wife had been at work. He didn't know what to do, for he didn't want to make a clamor unless the thing were better proven and more openly known. (Now the lady shall be deceived if she doesn't look out!)

Soon it was almost nightfall, and Aloul returned to his house. He didn't want his wife to see that he had discovered anything. The household sat down to eat by the fire, and after dinner they made up the beds. All the cowherds went to bed, and so did Aloul and his wife, together.

"Lady," he said, "you lie down first, over there next to the wall; for I am rising early to get the cowherds up. Then there will be time to go through the fields to reach our pastures."

"Sire, you go first," said the lady, "thank you. My hip hurts me here. I think a nail has risen up, for it is really causing me pain."

So Aloul appeased his wife by lying down first, and she after. But he did not guard her closely enough to prevent the gate from remaining open. Aloul was fooled, for he quickly fell asleep.

The priest came, step by step, straight to the gate, which he found unlatched. He pushed it a little, then opened it. Then he pissed all over it. But there was a bitch in the garden, making a great noise and barking. The priest did nothing else but go and piss on the trellis, for he didn't care about her noise.

When she saw and smelled the priest, she ran, or rather charged at him and seized him by the surcoat. It would have been too bad for him if he had remained outside then, but the priest rushed into the house. Softly he opened and closed the door, shutting out the noisy bitch. He hated the bitch and the danger she caused, for she never acted kindly toward men of his order, but wanted to chew and eat them.

Now the priest was inside the door, but it was after midnight, and he had delayed too long, for Aloul had been woken up. He had been much disturbed by a dream and was still shaken. For in his dream, it seemed to him that a priest, clipped and tonsured, had entered his bedroom and had surprised his wife, laid her beneath him, and worked his will; and Aloul was not able to aid her or harm him, until a cow began mooing and startled Aloul out of his delusion. But he was still in a great fright. He embraced and kissed his wife. He didn't want anyone to do him wrong. He took his beloved by the breast.

However, she was not asleep at all, but keeping watch. The priest did not delay; he came, step by step, straight to the bed where Aloul and his wife lay. She was in torment. She said, "I'm lying uncomfortably. Lift your arm that's resting on me. Move back; I've hardly any bed. I have barely enough room for my legs."

"God!" thought Aloul, "what does the woman want?"

Angrily he drew back, and the priest climbed on. They began making love. Aloul turned around and heard the bed creak, squeak, and shake. It seemed to him that some one was stealing from him. He was greatly worried about his wife, for she was not used to acting in this way.

He put his hand out beneath the sheets and felt the priest in her arms. He went on feeling him all over, barely able to keep silent. He seized the priest by his thing and pulled and tugged and shouted and cried, "Get up, get up, my people! Son of a bitch, get up, get up! Somebody or other has come in here and made me a cuckold with my wife."

The lady seized Aloul by the head and throat, trying to force him to release his fingers from around the priest's balls. He fell to the ground into the hearth in the middle of the room. Then the priest was master. He had suffered great pains, but who cares, when it's all for love, to do one's will?

Finally, the cowherds got up. One took a club, another a cudgel. If the priest hadn't moved, he would have had his neck battered. They were angry because their lord was shouting this way. The whole household arose, and everyone ran there. The priest had no retreat except the shed on the roof, where lambs were lying. There he hid and kept silent.

Then there was a great commotion in the bed between the lady and her husband, who was in despair over having wasted his effort. He could barely get his breath back, they had fought so much together. But the servants separated them, and the battle began again. Aloul drew out his sword and searched back and forth. There wasn't a bucket or a pail that the cowherds didn't move. But all of them knew very well that it was just a dream or a delusion. They didn't think anything had really happened.

"Sire," they said, "let all this be. Let's go rest and sleep. It was some dream or trick."

"Look in the valleys, look in the hills," said Aloul, who would not budge. "I held him in my own two hands, and what are you telling me? What? Is he going to get away free? Go look for him in that closet, and up and down the roof, and look under these stairs. Whoever can show him to me first will have served me well. He'll have two bushels of wheat at Christmas, besides his pay."

When the cowherds heard this they wanted the wheat, and began hurriedly going here and there, looking up and down everywhere. (If the priest isn't well hidden, he'll soon lose something.)

Well, there was in the house an old whore, Hersent, who was flabby and filthy. She went straight to the stable where the priest was hidden, without a lamp or candle. She shooed the lambs and woke them up, searching and groping around where the priest was crouched. His pants were down, and he had huge, swollen balls, which hung down to the ground. His ass was hairy; it seemed like some strange sort of face.

Hersent came there by chance, placing her hands on his balls, and thought that it was a sheep that she held in that place, by its great balls. She put her hands a little higher and found it hairy and round with a valley in the middle. Hersent drew back a little, wondering what it could be; and the other, watching (it's the priest) seized Hersent by the thighs. He dragged her back to him until his organ hung down to her ass, and joined himself to her.

Hersent was marvellously docile. She didn't know what to do. If she cried out, all the servants would come and know what had happened; so it was better for her to keep quiet. It wouldn't have done her any good to cry out. Hersent had to suffer everything he did to her whether she wanted to or not, without noise, cries, or shouting. She had to do it; it couldn't be avoided.

"Hersent," he said, "I'm the priest. I came here to your lady, but I was seen. Now I am in great peril. Hersent, look around and see if you can find a way for me to escape, and I swear to you on all my books that I will cherish you forever."

Hersent, who wasn't very happy, said, "Sire, don't be afraid. If I can manage it, you'll escape."

She got up and went off, pretending that she was angry, for she knew many ruses, and shouted in a loud voice: "Sons of bitches, boys, cowherds, what are you after? Go back to bed! Go back to bed, to your filthy mattresses! Don't you remember how my lady has labored for you, doing so much good for you? Whoever says this, speaks the truth: if you give a *villein* honor or do him a good deed, he hates you more than anything. That's the pay you get when you care about them.

"My lady has nothing to do with shamefulness. In fact, she's a very fine lady. She is renowned as a good woman, and here you are, giving her so much trouble. If I were in her place, there wouldn't be any eggs or cheese around here. You would pay for the damage and eat peas and bread. The person that named you *villeins* in the first place named you right. It's proper to call you *villeins*, for '*villein*' comes from 'villainy.' What are you looking for, you idiots? Why are you carrying on like this?"

When the cowherds heard Hersent and her threats, they were afraid that the insides of their stomachs would see no more cheese. They all gathered around to defend and excuse themselves.

"Hersent," they said, "it's our lord's doing; he makes us do what he wants. But from now on, none of us will have anything to do with it. We pledge ourselves to our lady, without making her swear anything; for she is both good and wise. Our lord has done her an outrage by wrongfully disbelieving her. Just listen to him; you can tell he's wrong. So let's go to bed."

All the cowherds returned to bed, while Aloul scolded his wife and told her not to do things which would bring him shame.

"God! I ought to be happy," said the lady, "for my lord gives me great honor! Cursed be such a marriage, and cursed my family that gave me to such a man! I cannot rest by day or at night or in the morning; and yet I know no reason, I see no reason why he should mistrust me. You're going to have plenty to do if you're going to watch over me all the time. You've got plenty of spying to do, prying into my deeds. You've taken on a real burden."

"Lady," he said, "let me be. I hope you never get any rest." He turned his back to her and pretended to sleep.

Then the priest, who couldn't stay put hidden in the roof-top stable, came back to the bed again and lay down with his beloved. Aloul, who wasn't sleeping at all, felt the priest get on; and thought to himself that while there were two of them, he was alone, and there were two of them. They could cause him trouble if they began a battle. Quietly he took hold of his sword, rose up and left them, and went back to his cowherds.

"Hey Rogier," he said, "are you sleeping? By my faith, he's come back, this fellow my wife has betrayed me with. This stranger wants to shame me. Wake up all your companions and let's go and attack him; and if we can capture the enemy by force, each one of you will have a cape or a coat and a belt to fit him."

Then each one pledged and swore when they heard the promise that they would sing him an asshole mass if they could get at him with their fists.

Hersent, who was not far off, had not gone to bed yet and was leaning against the doorway. She heard everything: what had happened, the complaint, and how Aloul was pursuing his shame. She went to the priest and told him about it. He was glad to hear this and be able to protect himself. He left there, but he took too long in getting away (which he would always regret), for he met Aloul halfway out.

"My God," said the priest, "imagine meeting you here!"

Aloul leaped and grabbed him quickly by the hair.

"Now," he said, "son of a bitch, everybody, lay into him! We'll hold him by force."

Then came the cowherds, hitting one, shoving the other, as if they were blind. They seized Aloul instead of the priest and beat his bones and nerves, all struggling to hold him. The priest jumped up and fled—he didn't know where, for it was night and he didn't know how to reach the gate. He would have happily abandoned the house; until suddenly, he found a club. He felt on the ground and found a flail which had been made that very year. The flail was long and wide, leaning against some steps. He took the flail and carried it up the stairs and through the door, planning to make a stand there. He knew what he would call his battletower if anyone came to him there.

Now the priest was in his fortress, and Aloul was in great distress, lying at the feet of his *villeins*; and they would certainly have treated him villainously if he had not quickly identified himself. He would have been treated worse than any bear in the pit if he had not called out his name. When they knew that it was their lord, they didn't know what to say. All of them were angry.

"Sire," they said, "are you wounded?"

"No," he said, "I've been worse off. But let's light a fire and get back to our agreement."

They lit a fire and went through the house, searching for the priest. Rogier, the master of them all, wished to serve his lord and climbed the stairs which the priest was guarding at the top. But Rogier, who wasn't being very careful, was going to get a beating. The priest took the flail he was holding and thrust and hit him with it so it cracked and broke. The priest came close and gave him such a blow on the back with his club that he shoved him down the stairs into the middle of the room. Then Rogier had what he was looking for. If Rogier didn't like it, it was too bad; that's my opinion. Who in his right mind goes hunting after madness?

Then Aloul came up with his servants. "Tell me," he said, "have you been hit?"

"Sire," he said, "I've been beaten up. My body and face are all banged up. Some Antichrist or other hit me on those stairs. He almost did me in. I think I'd better go lie down."

The cowherds went up the stairs. "By cock's ass, who is it?" They raised their sticks, wanting to know what it could be. They looked and saw the priest, leaning against the door, and saw the club he was holding. All of them drew back, for fear that he would hit them.

Aloul leapt forward with his sword drawn and went bravely toward him, infuriated. He climbed up three or four steps while the priest listened in silence. He said, "Who is it up there?"

"I am the priest up here, grieved and misled by fortune. Is it the fifteenth already? I thought it was Christmas. I'm very much afraid that this club may strike your neck. You would feel pretty foolish if you felt how much it weighed."

Then the great skirmish between the priest and the cowherds began again. Aloul, who was rather brave, approached the flail and broke off the better part of it with his sharp sword. When the priest saw that his fortress was being demolished, he swung his flail in that direction and hit Aloul with such vigor that he drove him down the stairs, so he couldn't have found any bread for sale. When he reached the ground he was so hurt and so confused that he couldn't say a single word.

"Aloul, this club is full of hornets," said the priest, "and I do believe they don't want us to come in their house. If one of the cowherds thinks he will have better luck, he can certainly come on up and enter. But if he loses some of his goods, don't let him come to me about it; for this castle is defending itself, and it's not well to climb up to it."

Then you could hear the cowherds swear by mountains, hills, and valleys that they would be so hot, discouraged, and weak that they could be flayed alive before they would give up trying to bring him down. Then the great war between the priest and the cowherds began again. The assault was fierce. All the cowherds assembled at the steps, troubled and angered for their lord. They piled benches and perches, chairs, ladders, and vine poles until they could reach the priest. But he defended himself so well from them that there was not a single one in the whole house, even protected and shielded, who was hardy enough not to be knocked down the ladder in spite of himself. They understood very well that if he could keep from being taken, he would cause them to live in dishonor and shame.

Then Robin climbed up. He was one of the strongest in the house. In his hand he held a club so large he could barely sustain it. Where there might be three hundred or a thousand men, there would be none so hardy as he. He was even somewhat better than Rogier, for he was more valiant. He would consider himself a traitor if he did not avenge his lord. (He it was that carried the drum at Sunday dances.)

He said not a word to the priest, but went forward. He struck out, hitting the priest with his club and making him turn to the right. Then he advanced, seized the priest by his hair, and drew him to him. The latter, who was afraid of losing his organ, rose up, clenched his teeth, and seized Robin by the loins, and dragged him to him with both hands. The other angrily pulled back. They held each other so tightly that you could have hauled them both quickly on a horse for two years.

The cowherds raised a shout. "Sire," they said, "let's climb up, take sticks, clubs, and cudgels, and go to the aid of our companion."

When the cowherds had assembled, they climbed up together. When the priest discovered that Robin was going to be aided, he strained and struggled. He pulled Robin to him so hard that he fell under him, and in spite of himself, he fell down the stairs, so that he felt as if his eyes had sprung out of his head.

Now they were all caught and couldn't hold on, but had to go down the stairs. They miscounted the steps as they clattered down. He threw those who had gone to the assault down backwards. They had all climbed up high and now saw that they had been mad. The steps fell on their necks, banging and beating them, battering their chests and heads, arms, flanks, and ribs. They counted every one of the steps on the way down. When they reached the ground, they fell together into the great, blazing fire. The ones underneath suffered great pains. They hurt their arms, their feet, their trunks and heads.

Now I shall tell you how the priest was distressed and deceived. When he had reached the ground, Sir Berengier seized him. (He was a villein, one of the cowherds. He used to drive out the mares. You have never seen anything like him. One eye squinted and the other was blind. He always looked sideways. One of his feet was straight, the other twisted.) He held the priest so fast by one of his feet that he couldn't go where he wanted. He shouted and cried out, "What are you doing, you cursed men? Come on, help

me castrate this priest. By the name of God, if he escapes, we'll all
have lost the capes he promised us, and the coats."

When the priest heard this, he pulled his leg away, freeing it
from Sir Berengier's hands; but he left behind his boot and his
surcoat as hostages. Better to leave his pledge behind than his
other thing. He saw he had no business there, got up, and left
them.

They all went running after him, swinging sticks and clubs. The
priest entered a storeroom and hung from the rafters, drawing his
knees up together, hiding so no one could find him. They came,
making a great noise, and entered the storeroom; but they didn't
find a single thing, not even the priest.

They wondered what this could be. It seemed like witchcraft.
The wisest of them didn't know what to say. They were sad and
discouraged. They all thought they had been bewitched by the
priest who had burned them. They were furious. They went out of
the storeroom to their lord and told him what had happened, that
the priest had got away.

"Got away, the devil!" said Aloul. "And I stay here, a cuckold,
not avenged by anybody! I am beginning to be sorry I ever met
that priest. If you want to be my friends, help me to spy on him
another time. Let's go to bed; for I am badly wounded in the side.
Cursed be that enemy who beat and wounded me! I'll never be
happy or joyful again if I don't avenge myself on him."

Aloul went back to bed, saying, "Sirs, keep watch in the courtyard and all around, for I think he is still in this manor. And if he
is hidden any place in the manor, you should find him."

"Sire, if we are lucky," said the cowherds; "but we need to eat,
for we have stayed up all night and worked quite a bit, and we're
all tired."

"That's all right," said Aloul, "go ahead, eat, all of you, if you
want. There is hardly any of the night left. You can easily watch it
out."

Then the cowherds went off and made a great fire to warm

themselves. They began talking of the priest and his adventure, muttering to each other, and when they had muttered, and spoken, and chatted, and retold the story enough, they began talking about eating. That is the way of the cowherd; he's never happy unless he has eaten.

Rogier, who carried the club, in charge of all the others in the house, ordered them to fetch some bacon to be roasted; and the pieces were to be wide and long, so that each would have enough. Berengier got up at Rogier's order and took a knife with a sharp steel edge. He went to the storeroom where the cured pigs were hanging from the beams.

Berengier felt around, searching for the fattest one; for he knew that the fattest made the best cooking. While he was feeling, he grasped the priest by the rump. In some places it felt soft, in others, hard. He thought it was rennet, which they used to hang up in such a way. He felt a little forward, then back, until he came to the knees. Then he thought he had found bones which had been put there to dry. He marvelled greatly at finding such a jumble.

He put his hand up and down and encountered the priest's prick. It was soft, and he didn't know what it could be—whether a scrap of meat or a sausage hung up to dry. This, he said to himself, he would cut off; for it was a fine morsel. The priest could tell that the knife was coming close to his genitals if he didn't come down; so, all at once, he fell on Berengier, breaking and shattering his bones. He almost stabbed his neck.

Then Berengier thought he would go mad, returning without the bacon. He went back to the fire with one arm broken. "Noble cowherds," he said, "help me to hang the pig back up. The rope broke and it fell down. The fall almost broke my neck. Damn the butcher who hung it up!"

They took lights and lit up the house. Berengier led them to look at the pig and see how it had fallen. But when they came to the storeroom they didn't find it, or anything else. The pigs were hanging, as before, from the beams, all twenty, not one out of place. Everybody began laughing. One said that Berengier was scared to go near the pigs, and another said he was probably afraid of the priest.

"Sirs," he said, "enough of this. We can let this be. But I tell you the truth when I say I felt a pig fall on me, or maybe a ham. There was rennet with it, and it was soft and hard. What could that be?"

"I think," they said, "that it's the priest. Berengier felt his feet when he was hiding from us up there. Let's look around to see if he isn't here."

Berengier looked and saw the priest near a door, but the obscurity of the night prevented him from seeing him clearly. He began feeling for the priest; but the priest, when he noticed that Berengier saw and felt him, knew he was found. He struck him with his great, square fist between his neck and his hat so that he was knocked off his feet.

"Go, Sir Berengier," he said, "you have your pay. Turn and arise, for you are now absolved. I can give you no other pardon. Have your companions come and they shall take part in this offering. He is a fool who asks for foolish counsel. I hardly think you are wise to bear such a message. You took up the challenge to perform and accomplish that old bumble-bee's will. Have your companions come, and they shall receive their portion of this blessing."

Then from everywhere cowherds came in a great swarm. (The priest will have a bad lesson if he doesn't defend himself!) Rogier leapt at him first and seized him by the right hand, but the priest struck back with his left hand so hard that he was hurt and vanquished. Rogier would have been badly off if it hadn't been for the crowd of cowherds shoving and hurting him. There was such a press of cowherds that they filled the storeroom, but they were afraid of the club which he had used before.

They caused such a noise and commotion that their lord, Aloul, was awakened, wondering what all the noise was about. Then as he listened, he heard and understood that it was the priest and his friends who were at it again. He jumped to his feet, seized his sword, and headed straight for the battle. When he came to the assault, he jumped right in among the cowherds and seized the priest from behind. He, in turn, hit him in the face, knocking him down onto a cowherd. But how could he delay being captured now? He was assailed from all sides and his defense was useless.

They took him and all held on to him, in case the assault should begin again. Aloul asked his cowherds whether he should kill him there or hang him. They all replied together that there was no revenge worth speaking of except cutting off his balls.

"Cut them off . . . no. . . ." said Aloul. "Or rather, yes, slice them off. You say the truth, and I'll follow your advice. Go look for the razor to castrate this priest. Do it quickly, now."

When the priest heard what was being said about him, he spoke gently to Aloul. "Aloul," he said, "for the love of God, do not disfigure me in this way. Have compassion on the sinner."

"I shall never make any deals with you," said Aloul; "not for money."

If the priest was frightened then, it's easy to understand why. They brought the razor and threw down and beat up the priest. They thrashed and cursed him until they could get him down. They brought a log to ease his legs.

"Whoever knows how to help best, come and take the razor."

"I will, sire," said Berengier. "In fact, I would have cut them off a lot sooner."

They pulled down his pants; Berengier kneeled down and took the priest by the balls. Then the priest would have been in a real mess; but the lady, having stirred up the fire, came running with her maid. She found before her a huge chair; and, being strong and sturdy, she struck Berengier in the back with it, knocking him

over and almost killing him. Hersent took up a staff and beat him
in the rear, which was fat all over. The cowherds stood back from
the great blows they were giving. Both of them raised such a
skirmish that they threw the priest, free, out of the house.

He fled away, you can be sure, exhausted and beaten and vanquished. He had really fallen into bad hands. His hair stood on
end and the tatters of his coat and surcoat hung down to the
ground. He had left his boot as a pledge and escaped in great peril,
for he had been in harsh exile.

Notes to "Aloul"

"Aloul" is in many ways as pure an example of a fabliau as can
be found. There is the standard love affair between the wife of a
bourgeois and a priest, there are ruses and trickery galore, and
there is the almost successful emasculation at the end. The author
lets it be known that he is decidedly for the lovers and against the
cuckold, though the course of his story allows the husband a
momentary triumph. "Aloul" is part of a long tradition criticizing
jealous husbands and defending faithless wives. The author even
uses the classic argument that wives are faithless *because* their
husbands are jealous, thus shifting the blame rather neatly from
culprit to victim.

Although it is common enough for the *fableor* to side with the
erring wife, in the majority of cases he denounces her either ex-
plicitly or by implication. The belief that jealous husbands pro-
duce faithless wives is also prevalent in noble circles, where it
forms a part of courtly love doctrine.*

* I am perfectly aware of recent criticisms of this term, but I disagree with
them. While recognizing that C. S. Lewis' analysis of courtly love was un-
sound in many respects, it still seems to me that a fairly consistent pattern of
thought runs through much medieval literature which can most appropriately
be labelled "courtly love."

Nothing in the author's attitudes requires him to be either noble or bourgeois, but his style reveals him to have been fully familiar with aristocratic literature. No other fabliau contains such a wealth of literary parody, borrowing conventions of epic and romance. The priest's seduction of the wife in the beginning is a delightful parody of courtship scenes in noble romances, complete with the standard vocabulary, and the situation and social class of the lovers turns this idyll into a farce. Aloul's dream imitates the prophetic dreams of epics, and, further, the battle between the cowherds and the priest is described in epic terms from beginning to end, with an effect impossible to convey precisely in translation.

It might be suggested that this parody is a product of bourgeois humor, ridiculing the literature of the upper classes; but as far as we know, commoners enjoyed epics and romances quite as much as the nobility evidently enjoyed fabliaux. As a matter of fact, the "noble" genres are not maligned by this parody. "Aloul" belongs rather to the class of antibourgeois satire in which the noble author mocks his social inferiors by contrasting them with knights and epic heroes. Aloul and the priest are made ridiculous by the comparison with noble warriors and lovers, not vice versa.

For contrast, there is the following tale of nocturnal misadventures—a "bourgeois" tale of almost classic purity—told with a skill uncommon even in distinctively aristocratic narratives, "The Sacristan Monk."

- ruses, trickery
- love affair betw. bourgeois wife + a priest

The Sacristan Monk

I shall tell you the life of a monk, the sacristan of the abbey, who loved a townswoman who was good and courteous. Her name was Ydoine, and her husband was Guillaume, the money changer. Ydoine was well brought up, courteous, and nicely groomed. Guillaume did his money changing well, determined to make a great deal. He was good and courteous, but he didn't like barroom meals. He didn't hang around taverns, and his house was nice and neat. He didn't keep the breadbox latched; it was open to everyone. If a bum asked him for something of his, he gave it willingly. He was a marvellously rich man.

But the devil, who keeps eternal watch, set about to trick them and bring them to poverty. He would borrow from Guillaume, and he would not be able to carry on his money changing. At fair time Guillaume went to Provins and brought back eighty pounds of fine provisions. He returned through Amiens and bought clothing, then went off, happy to have done such good business.

But thieves were watching the paths and roads. His companions went off, and he followed two days later because he was celebrating too joyously. He had not gone far before he entered the forest where the thieves were, robbing merchants. When they saw Guillaume coming, they came from all directions to seize him.

Source: T. B. W. Reid, ed., *Twelve Fabliaux* (Manchester, Eng.: Manchester University Press, 1958), pp. 34–53.

They knocked him off his horse, but did him no other harm, except to take away his money belt.

Then they saw his assistant following him down the path, leading his greyhounds. The three thieves ran up to him and cut him to pieces with their knives. When Guillaume saw him die, he began to flee, escaping on foot. He had hardly gained a profit. Those who had entrusted him with their goods, thinking they would get them back when he returned to the market said, "This is a piece of bad business. What have you done with our money? Return it immediately."

Guillaume said to his neighbors, "Sirs, I still have three grain mills; all of them mill flour. Don't all of you be angry with me. Take them, leave me in peace, until I have reestablished myself." He gave it to them and they went off, paid to their satisfaction.

He went home to his wife, that courteous lady. Because he saw she was angry, he spoke to her gently and said, "Ydoine, my love, for God's sake do not be angry. Our Lord has consented that I should lose my goods, so that is as it should be. He will give us his counsel, if He wills."

She replied, "Of course, my dear. For the love of God, I do not know what to say. Our loss grieves me, and the assistant who was killed has met an ill fate. But I do not care, as long as you are alive, for you can recover your losses; but the dead cannot be restored."

That was all that happened that night. The next day about noon, Ydoine went to the abbey to pray to the son of Saint Mary, for whom the church was founded. She lit a candle that the Lord God might counsel her and give her lord profits. She put her candle on the altar, and from her eyes, which seemed like stars, she wept. She sighed so from her heart that she could not say her prayer.

The sacristan, who had long loved her, watched her, then came forward and greeted her: "Lady, welcome. I am delighted to see you."

She was not embarrassed, but wiped her eyes and answered,

"May God bless and keep you, Sire." Then she said gently, "How are you, Sire?"

"Well, my lady," said the sacristan, "I could wish for nothing more nor less than to have you with me in a secret bed. Then I would achieve what I have long desired. I am the treasurer here, and I will give you very good pay. You shall have one hundred pounds from me, and you will be able to live well."

When Ydoine heard him speak of one hundred pounds, she began to consider whether she would take them or not; for one hundred pounds is a fine gift. But she truly loved Guillaume, her lord, and said to herself, "I shall not take them without his leave."

The monk spoke to her again: "Lady, by our gown, I have great care because of you. You have caused me to suffer for a long time. I have loved you for four years. Of course, I never touched you with my hand, but now I shall touch you."

Then he embraced and kissed her by force. Ydoine pulled back and said, "Good sir, you should not make love in the church. I shall go to my house and speak with my lord and ask for his counsel."

Said the monk, "I'm amazed that you would seek counsel from him."

She told him, "Don't be afraid. People do many things for gain. I think I can lie to my lord in such a way that I shall do your will."

The monk took out an alms purse with ten sous in it and gave it to her. Ydoine gladly took them. She went home, where there was neither bread nor salt, for she was tormented by poverty and the loss that Sir Guillaume had suffered in the forest.

She spoke, while he remained silent. "Sire," she said, "listen to me. Let me give you a piece of advice which I think will make you rich within two years."

"Lady," he said, "in what way?"

Then Ydoine pulled out the alms purse which the monk had

given her, quickly opened it, and gave it to him with ten sous in it. Guillaume gladly took it.

Then she said to him, "My dear, for God's sake do not be angry if I tell you a secret." And she told him from beginning to end how the monk had courted her when he found her in the church, and how he had promised her one hundred pounds. Guillaume listened to this and laughed, saying that for all the treasure of Octavian or Nebuchadnezzar he would not allow any man living to make carnal love to her. He would rather seek his bread in the countryside or die of hunger.

When Ydoine heard this, she replied, "Sire, if we could find some way to trick the sacristan, we could get his money, and I think that would be a good thing. He would never complain to the prior or the abbot."

He replied, "That's no joke. I would be happy if we could have those coins. It's a great undertaking. What advice would you give?"

"Sire," she said, "I shall tell you. Listen to what I will do. Tomorrow morning I shall go to the church, straight to the altar of Saint Martin, and speak with the sacristan. If I can find him, I will tell him to come to me and keep the agreement he offered me. He will keep it; I know very well he will come, carrying with him a moneybelt full of coins."

"Lady," he said, "we shall see. Cursed he who hesitates!"

"True," said the lady, "I agree."

"Lady," he said, "it is late. It's time to think about eating our dinner."

"Sire," she said, "you are right. Go buy whatever kind of meat you wish." And she gave him the ten sous.

Guillaume went to the shops, bought plenty of bread and meat, and returned to the house. Ydoine called a boy to go for wine, pepper, and cummin, making the sauce herself. Then they sat down in love together—themselves and the boy alone—and se-

cretly dined. When they had eaten and drunk, they went to bed
and kissed and embraced. That night they did not speak of
poverty and suffering, for they were content in each other's arms.

In the morning at dawn Ydoine got dressed and put on her
shoes. When she was dressed and adorned, her hair wrapped in a
silk wimple, she went straight to the church. The mass had already
been chanted before she entered, and the people who had heard
the mass were coming out of the church. Ydoine went forward,
straight to the altar of Saint Martin, and stopped to pray.

The monk came to look around, to see when she would come.
He was overjoyed when he saw her. He came forward and said,
"Your delay has greatly grieved me. Now tell me your will, for my
heart is on fire for you. I have not eaten or drunk since I spoke to
you yesterday morning."

She said, "Do not be dismayed; be reassured, for this very night
you shall do your delight with me in my bed, if you keep your
agreement with me."

The monk quickly replied, "Lady, don't be afraid. I will bring
one hundred pounds or more. I've got good reason to bring them;
for if I can sport with you, I neither desire nor demand anything
else, by the faith which I owe God Omnipotent."

He gave her enough coins to purchase food. Then they took
their leave of each other and went off. He thought of his affair and
went to search the boxes and chests and the altars at the reli-
quaries, where people who had heard the service had put their
offerings. He filled a large money belt with it. He hadn't lied, for
there were at least one hundred pounds in it. In fact, if he could,
he would willingly have put more in it. The scoundrel joyfully
headed for his misadventure.

Ydoine did not delay to prepare something to eat. Guillaume
ate first and lay down in his bed to beat the monk. He held a club
which he had borrowed from a servant. When the monks had
heard and sung complines, they went to lie down in the dormitory,

but the monk remained in the chapel. He didn't go to bed at all, but thought of his beloved. He secretly and quietly slipped out through a postern gate and headed straight for Guillaume's house where his suit was to be granted.

He went to the door, called out, and Ydoine opened and closed it behind him. Now they were both in the house, and Guillaume was lying in the bed. The monk ate and drank privately with his mistress, who was to be dearly bought.

She said, "My darling love, where is what you promised me?"

He replied, "Lady, take this moneybelt and keep it. There are one hundred pounds in it. I wouldn't lie to you for anything."

Ydoine went to store them away and saw the keys which he had dropped by the fire, thrown on the bench. Ydoine was lovely and gentle, and her beauty tormented the monk. He rose up and wanted to do it with her by the warm fire. But she said, "For the love of God, both of us would be shamed! I'm afraid people passing on the street would see us. Carry me into that chamber, and there you can do your will."

When the monk heard her, he got up, grieved that she was delaying things, and quickly took her to the chamber and threw her across the bed on her back. Guillaume jumped on and said, "Monk, by Saint Paul, I think you're crazy to want to shame my wife. I would be miserable if I permitted it, and God cannot will her to consent."

The monk heard him and got up, wanting to seize him, but the other gave him such a blow with the club that he was stunned. Once the monk was stunned, Guillaume struck again, hitting him in the back of the head so that his brains splattered, and the monk fell forward. Thus does a fool go seeking his death.

When Ydoine saw him die, she let out a sigh from her heart. "Alas, misery," said Ydoine. "I wish I were in Babylon, unhappy wretch! Curse the day I was born, to have such a thing happen because of me. Guillaume, why did you do it?"

"Lady," he said, "he was so big that I was afraid he would seize me in his arms. Would you have liked to have felt his solace between your legs, then? The only thing we can do now is flee, go into some foreign land so far away that no one will know us or look for us."

"Sire," she said, "we cannot. I shall tell you why: the gates of the town are closed and the guards are standing watch over them."

Ydoine wept; Guillaume thought; and he who had thought like a fool lay quite still. When Guillaume had thought for a while, he raised his head and said, "Ydoine, my love, how did he come from the abbey?"

"Sire," she said, "through the postern gate which opens into the enclosure. I saw the keys on that bench."

Guillaume took a white cloth and bound up the monk's head, lifting his neck. He took up the monk (he ought to have cut his throat!) and Ydoine followed him out, not to remain there alone, and went and sat by a window.

Guillaume was able to handle this well. He came to the postern gate that the monk had come out of, and put him down, opened the gate, and picked him up again. Guillaume entered a pathway by which the monks went to piss. He went straight to the room where they cured themselves of the bellyache and entered it. He sat down on the first hole, looked toward the door, and saw a load of hay which the monks used to wipe their buttocks on their way out of the room. Guillaume was no fool. He made a wiper out of it, stuck it in the priest's fist, then went off down an old street. He was sweating all over from fear.

He found his wife Ydoine terribly frightened. They entered their house together and comforted each other, for they thought they were delivered of the monk whom they had killed.

The monk sat with his mouth hanging open, for he had had a mortal blow. The others were in the dormitory. The prior of the abbey lay in a bed next to the refectory. He had eaten too much and could not delay any longer; he had to go empty himself some-place. He entered the room and stopped at the first hole, to empty himself as soon as possible. As he was beginning to force himself along, he raised his head and saw the dead sacristan, who was not moving his hands or feet.

"Aha!" he said, "This sacristan is a villain, sleeping here. It won't be wrong if he pays for it tomorrow when we are in the chapter. He couldn't have done worse if he had been absent at the reading of the epistles."

He went forward to wake him up. "Sir sacristan," said the prior, "it would be better to sleep in the dormitory than here in the latrine. Shame on your gain, which has brought you such shame! I would have had my thighbone broken and my back burned by a hot fire before I would sleep in such a vile place."

When he had done what he wanted, he went up to the sacristan and said, "Sir sacristan, wake up." But he, who was quite dead, fell down across the privy. When the prior saw him fall, he said, "What's this, by the Holy Spirit? This man is dead. I was wrong to get involved with him. I wish I'd never come this way. God, how should I be counselled? He argued with me the day before yesterday, and I with him, it's true. They'll tell the abbot that I treacherously murdered him."

The prior was stupefied, wondering what he could do, how he could get out of this. He said to himself that he would carry him out into the town and leave him at the door of some towns-woman—the loveliest and most courteous in the entire fief. People would say the next day that someone there had killed him. He took the monk up and laid him across his shoulder, then he turned and carried him to the house where the monk had received the poison from which he would never recover. (Now I pray that Guillaume will be careful. If anyone finds him there in the morning, I think he will be near his end.)

Guillaume and Ydoine lay by each other, greatly frightened,

comforting each other. Then a gust of wind blew the clothes of the monk, lifting them up and moving them so that they struck the door.

Ydoine said, "By Saint Audomarus, Sir Guillaume, get up. There is someone at our door. He's been spying on us tonight."

Guillaume got up, took his club, went swiftly to the door and opened it; and the dead monk fell on his chest and Guillaume fell on his back. When Guillaume fell down, he wondered what had happened. He shouted out to his wife, "Ydoine, come and help me. Somebody has fallen on top of me. May God curse me, if it's a man and I don't kill him."

Ydoine jumped up stark naked, ran to the fire, lit it, saw the monk and said, "Guillaume, we are betrayed. It's the sacristan lying here."

"Lady," he said, "you're right. A curse on evil wealth, greed, and treachery, for nothing but evil comes from it! But isn't he dead?"

"Yes, certainly."

Both of them marveled greatly and said that it was the devil that had brought him back. Guillaume took him up again. Ydoine gave him a note with the name of God written on it. He gladly took it, for he trusted in it.

He went off with the monk and came to the dungheap of Sir Tibout, the tenant farmer, who took care of the monk's wheat. He had a pot full of coins and other riches besides. He had a large bacon from a pig he had killed, which he had fattened in his house for the whole season, then hung up to dry. A bum had stolen it the day before and hidden it in Sir Tibout's dungheap. He didn't know any other way out.

Guillaume, carrying the monk, stopped on the dungheap. He was exhausted from having carried him through the town. He tried to think by what trick he could best get rid of him. He decided to bury him in the dung of the dungheap and leave him.

He put the monk down and made a large hole with his hand to bury the sacristan. He felt the bacon which the thief had buried and was startled. He saw that the skin was black, and he began to be frightened.

Guillaume said to himself, "For sure, there's another black monk here—plenty black, I think. Well, let's put them both together." He wanted to do it, but he couldn't.

"What is this, by the Baron Saint Lot?" Guillaume saw he couldn't do it. Then he thought he would look and see what monk it was that had been killed. He moved the pig. "God's grace," he said, "it's meat! Now I haven't completely lost the cart load that was taken from me in the forest. I've got money and food in plenty."

He put the monk in the sack and began covering him over. When everything was as it had been before, he went running off with the pig and returned home.

When his wife saw him loaded down, she asked, "Is that the sacristan?"

"No, not at all, lady, by Saint Germain. It's a big, fat pig. We have meat; go look for some cabbages."

The fellow who had taken the pig from the *villein*, as I said, was gambling in a tavern. He had wine, but couldn't drink it. He said to his companions, "Lords, what shall we do? I think if we had a fat pig to roast we would drink much better."

All swore by their eyes, "Good friend, that's the truth! But we can't get any. The butchers are asleep, and besides, we don't have a cent."

"Sirs," he said, "I have a fine one which I will present to you. It's big and fat. I stole it, and I'll gladly give it to you. It's at Sir Tibout's, the tenant farmer, hidden in a dungheap."

"Go get it," they said, "and hurry."

He who had stolen many things went straight to the dungheap

where he had stashed the bacon. He lifted the monk by the neck and carried him to the tavern.

Everyone shouted, "Welcome!" He threw down his load, saying to them, "Lords, it's plenty heavy." Then they called out Cortoise, the chambermaid of the inn. "Say," they said, "tell us where the spit is. We want to roast some meat. Are these dishes washed? Hurry up, and we'll go look for some firewood around here."

She followed their orders, and they rushed off to a palisade which was made of large stakes. Each of them pulled one out and turned back. They asked for a quince, and she gave it to them. She washed the pan and ran to the sack. Like a fool, she opened it and seized the monk by the boot. She wanted to slice it, but she couldn't.

"Look at that girl making a mess," said the thieves. "She's not doing a thing." The maid heard them and answered back, "By Saint Leonard, this bacon is tougher than a willow branch. I do believe it has shoes on."

All of them jumped up. "Shoes on!" they said. "How?"

She showed them the monk in the sack, and the one who had carried him crossed himself I don't know how many times.

"Hey, Guarnot," said the innkeeper, "why did you kill this monk?"

"Sire," he said, "you're mistaken. Never did I touch him, by all the saints! I know, it's the devil who's made a monk out of the pig. May God give me confession, it was a pig I took. The devil has disguised himself as a monk to trick us. But I know how to get us out of this. I'll carry him to Sir Tibout's."

"Go then," they said, "hurry up. And hang him from the rafter where you took the pig."

"That's what I'll do, by Saint Denis."

He took up the monk, lifted him onto his shoulder, and went out into the street. Then he saw a big old cart lying in a garden. Guarnot leaned it up against the house and climbed up it to the hole he had made when he had taken out the pig. He shoved it right through the middle and hung it up by a cord tight around the neck. He went quickly back to the ground and returned to the tavern to tell his companions how he had hung the monk up by the cord where the pig had been.

Now let us leave off talking about the thieves. I want to tell you about the peasant [Tibout], who was lying with his wife. She began waking him up. "Sire," she said, "it's morning already, and a good time to go to the mill, for we have only two loaves of bread."

"Lady," the peasant answered, "I've been sick for three days. Wake up Martin; he'll go. He's that peddler who sleeps here twice or three times a month. Promise him a loaf."

"Sire," she said, "that's fine with me."

Then she said, "Martin, get up."

"Lady," he said, "why should I?"

"You have to go to the mill."

"Lady," he said, "you're kidding. You killed your pig, and never forced me to eat anything from its bones or bowels. Am I your servant, just because I lie on your straw mattress? Any peasant in the country will lend me or gladly give me just as much as you do here."

"Martin," she said, "don't complain, and I'll give you a roasted slice of my bacon and bread to eat with it. Can you find it in yourself to do what I want?"

"Lady," he said, "gladly. I'll do whatever you want."

"Martin," she said, "you should have some of it, and you will have it."

Then she hit her husband. "Sire," she said, "get up. Go to the pig and cut off a slice for Martin, and he'll go straight to the mill."

The peasant climbed up to his storeroom. "Where do you want me to cut it from?"

"Sire, where you like. It's stupid to ask for advice about it. It's more yours than mine."

"My faith," said Tibout, "you're right. Light the fire so I can see."

"By my faith, sire, I won't. You know perfectly well where it's hanging."

Sir Tibout reached out his hand, thinking to seize the pig, but took the monk by the heel. He wanted to cut a slice off it. But the cord was dry and smoky, and it broke, and the "pig" fell, hitting Sir Tibout on the head and knocking him to the bottom of the old trough. When Sir Tibout felt that he had fallen down, he shouted loudly for Martin. "Martin," he said, "get up! The pig has fallen on me!"

Then Martin got up, ran and lit the fire, and angrily looked at the monk. He crossed himself more than thirty times. "Sire, sire," said Martin, "by the faith I owe Saint Martin, it's not a pig; it's a villain who looks like a tonsured monk. And he's got shoes on, may God save me! The pig that was hanging up isn't here at all; we've lost it. We have a monk for our pig."

"Alas," said Tibout, "now I'm dead. Tomorrow I'll be wrongly hung, for everybody will say tomorrow that I've killed the sacristan."

"Sire, sire," said Martin, "lamenting isn't worth a leek. Think of some way to carry the monk back to the abbey where he came from. Then the one who put us in this mess will hang from a gallows or from that birch tree."

"Martin," said the peasant, "go and bring me my colt. I'll tie the knight on him. I think I'll make him a knight."

Martin brought the colt and worked hard to tie him tightly into the stirrups. Martin said, "By Saint Climent, I'll bring a lance, and he'll go jousting in the courtyard. You shout out that he's getting away, stealing: 'Help! Help! The sacristan is leading my colt off by force!' "

Then they shoved the colt out and the peasant cried, "Help! Help!" loud and long. Hundreds of people followed the monk, thinking he was out of his mind. The colt wandered until it entered the gate. The sacristan, bearing a shield, met the subprior, who had risen too early, and struck him with his lance, throwing him from his palfrey. Everyone marvelled and shouted together, "Wretches! Run, turn around! The sacristan's gone mad! Whoever waits for him will be killed!"

Then neither weak nor strong remained there; they went and locked themselves up. The colt jumped into the kitchen, smashing buildings, pots, bowls, mortars, plates, and platters. He wildly flung the shield at the walls more than a hundred times until the lance was shattered. Then the noise quieted down, and the colt wandered off.

He came to a ditch and jumped so furiously over the wide ditch that all the saddlegirths broke, and everything—monk and horse—fell in a heap to the bottom of the ditch. They pulled him out with an iron hook. The monk didn't cry or shout, for he had been dead for quite a while.

Thus Guillaume revenged himself on the monk who had thought he could deceive his wife with his money. He got the pig and one hundred pounds. And thus Guillaume got off free, for he was never accused. And thus Sir Tibout lost his bacon and his colt. Thus the sacristan was killed.

Notes to "The Sacristan Monk"

Le Moine segretain presents an interesting variation on the priest-as-cured-pig motif we found in "Aloul," besides sharing other traits with that tale. Aloul and Guillaume (before the robbery) belong to approximately the same social class, and their wives become involved with priests for whom their husbands lay traps. Yet "The Sacristan Monk" is a distinctively different story from "Aloul." Guillaume is not a jealous old man, but a quite sympathetic husband. Although it is not quite clear just what his wife has in mind at every point in the story, for in the scene with the priest she seems to think that she might be able to persuade Guillaume to accept the offer (Is Guillaume perhaps justified when he rebukes her as she laments the priest's death?), she loves her husband, unlike the wife of Aloul. She and Guillaume plot to trap the priest together.

The tone of the story seems to me distinctively bourgeois. One feels the despair of Guillaume at losing his merchandise and understands his agreement to cooperate with a rather degrading ruse. The author extols Guillaume's good bourgeois virtues of industry, sobriety, and thrift combined with a becoming measure of charity.

The skill of the author does not argue against this conclusion. His exquisitely plotted slapstick would probably be beyond the capabilities of a writer tied to aristocratic conventions, and it evidences a peculiarly bourgeois sort of excellence. The concluding scene, with the dead monk disguised as a knight, seems to verge on parody, but here it is not an antibourgeois satire, but an anticlerical one characteristic of the lower classes. The only positive hint of antibourgeois satire is the humorous use of noble titles applied to commoners, but that is hardly very significant.

Accepting the fact that the work is written from a bourgeois point of view and for the bourgeoisie, it nevertheless seems possible that it was enjoyed by the nobility. It was, in fact, an immensely popular tale. There are no less than five distinct versions, one quite different from the others, and even more bourgeois in character, called *Dou prestre comporte ou La longue nuit*. The central motif of the story is that of "the body many times killed," which has a long and honorable history. It would be surprising if the upper classes were ignorant of "The Sacristan Monk."

To conclude this collection there is a unique little work called "The Lay of the Lecher." It is not actually a lay, but purports to be an account of how lays are written.

- bourgeois tone
- priest-as-cured-pig motif
- anticlerical: dead monk disguised as a knight

- motif: "the body many times killed"

The Lay of the Lecher

In olden times, the Bretons tell us, on Saint Pantelion's Day many people—the noblest and the most beautiful in the land—used to gather to honor that saint's feast. No woman worth anything failed to attend. The gathering was splendid; everyone put all his effort into dressing and adorning himself.

A contest was held here, and tales were told of love affairs and deeds of chivalry. Whatever had happened to anyone was soon heard and remembered; they told their tales and the others listened. They remembered, told, and retold the best of the tales. It was told and recounted until everyone had praised it. Then they made a lay together; this was their custom. They gave it the name of the person to whom the adventure had happened. That is the truth; the lay was named after him.

Then the lay was carried on until it was known everywhere; for those who could play the viol, the harp, or the lute carried it out of that land to the realms where they went.

At the feast I am speaking of, where the Bretons gathered, the assembly was held on a high hill so that they could hear better. There were many clerks and knights and many people of other trades. There were ladies, noble and lovely, and maidens and girls.

Source: Gaston Paris, ed., "Lais inédits de Tyolet, de Guingamor, de Doon, du Lecheor et de Tydorel," *Romania*, VIII (1879): 29–72.

When they had come out of the church, they went and assembled together at the place they had chosen. Each one told his deed, each told his adventure, one after another. Then they prepared to choose who should win.

Eight ladies sat off to one side and gave their own opinion. They were the flower of the prowess and valor of Bretagne.

One spoke first, and said boldly, "Ladies, give me your counsel on a matter at which I marvel greatly. I have heard these knights speak a great deal of tourneying and jousting, of adventures, of love affairs, and of pleading with their beloveds. But so far there has been no talk of the thing for which all these great things are done.

"For what are they good knights? Why do they love to fight in tourneys? For what do the young men adorn themselves? For what do they put on new clothes? To what do they send their jewels, their treasures, and their rings? For what are they noble and debonaire? Why do they keep from doing wrong? Why do they like to woo, to kiss and embrace?

"Do you know any reason besides one single thing? Otherwise none of them would woo so much, nor speak and plead finely. If that should go away, they would not want to continue doing these things. This is the source of the great delights for which honorable deeds are done. Many men are improved and made worthy and good who wouldn't be worth a button if it weren't for the desire for cunt.

"I pledge you my faith, no woman has such a pretty face that she could have a friend or lover if she had lost her cunt. Since all good things are done for it, let us not prize anything else. Let us make the new lay of cunt; then we shall hear of something really fine. Whoever knows how to play, begin; you shall see everyone turn toward us."

The other seven agreed and said that she had spoken well. Then they began the lay, each adding her voice and sweet, high notes.

The lay was courteous and fine. All those who were at the festival left off the lays they were making and turned toward the ladies. They praised them highly and made the lay together with them, when they heard the fine subject matter. The lay was kept and cherished by both clerks and knights. It was greatly loved and brought great joy; it was never disliked at all.

Most people say that this is the "Lay of the Lecher." I don't wish to say the right name, so no one will take me wrong. According to the story I have heard, I have now finished the lay for you.

Notes to "The Lay of the Lecher"

The literature of courtly romance is filled with the praise of the power of love. All tournaments, all battles, all adventures are for the sake of love. Lancelot's love for Guinevere is a classic example of the idea that the love of noble ladies inspires the best men to great deeds. Loving a good woman not only makes a man more valorous, it makes him more polite, more generous, more attractive, and improves him in every way. It is the idea vulgarized in the nineteenth century to "woman purifies man."

Yet in the majority of cases, this love is no purely spiritual affair. Knights go to bed with their mistresses; Lancelot certainly goes to bed with Guinevere. The driving power behind this complex force called courtly love was sex, and everyone knew it. Still, it was seldom put so bluntly. The language of courtly love is full of euphemisms and evasions.

The author of *Le Lai du lecheor* has a single, simple point to make. The narrators of romances and lays always praise knightly prowess, but everyone knows that their prowess depends on the power of love, and the power of love is nothing other than the power of cunt. So let us praise cunt.

Nothing could more clearly demonstrate that the lords and ladies who read and heard epics and romances were quite as capable as their bourgeois countrymen of realism and honesty, and, lest we forget, capable of laughing at themselves.